NIGHTMARE'S
END

NIGHTMARE'S END

C. SMITH

"The fury of a demon instantly possessed me. I knew myself no longer."
— Edgar Allan Poe, *"The Black Cat"*

PART ONE
Ava

PART ONE
Ava

CHAPTER ONE

The sound of teeth chattering pulled my attention away from the closed door. Carrie Johnson stood next to me, her clammy hand grasping my arm as if her life depended on it — which it might. She'd moved in a few weeks ago with her husband, Nathan, and their twin toddlers, Allie and Riley. I received an email from Carrie two days ago asking me to get rid of a poltergeist that had been causing too much chaos for her liking.

Now here we stood: Carrie pallid and violently shaking, looking ready to bolt at any moment, and me, trying my best to remain calm and collected. On the inside, I was screaming like a scared little girl. Needless to say, this was no poltergeist — my mere presence appeared to anger it even more.

I took a deep, calming breath as I slowly opened the door. The musty scent of the cellar replaced the sweet aroma of Carrie's floral perfume. Although I saw nothing but darkness as I peered down the stairs, I knew *he* was down there. The steady creaking of old wood drifted up to us eerily, instantly raising the hair on the nape of my neck.

"Y-you're not going down there, are you?" Carrie whispered shakily. I flinched ever so slightly as her fingernails dug into my arm.

I nodded as I held a finger up to my lips. Her frightened brown eyes were begging me to not go. I motioned for her to stay put before carefully placing my foot on the first step.

The loose wooden step creaked under my foot. *Damn these old houses,* I thought. There was no way I'd make it down without being heard. Hesitantly, I took the next step, then another, and another. Although I reached the bottom of the old, janky staircase within seconds, it felt much longer.

The steady creaking sound continued, louder now. I looked straight ahead and squinted, but it was too dark to see anything. The light switch was at the top of the stairs, but I'd decided against turning it on in fear of giving away my presence. *I'm sure the stairs took care of that.* I rolled my eyes at the thought.

Figuring my presence was already well-known, I pulled my cell phone out of my back pocket to use as a flashlight. Keeping the light aimed toward the ground, I tiptoed forward. As I walked deeper into the cellar, another sound joined the creaking: humming.

I listened intently, trying to make out the tune. It wasn't anything I recognized — if it was even a real song at all. I took a few more baby steps forward then stopped. Trying to will my hand to stop shaking, I slowly aimed the light straight ahead.

There he was — moving back and forth in an old rocking chair, his back to me. His jet-black hair was sticking out in every direction. Through the back of the chair, I could tell he still had on the button-down shirt and slacks he wore to work earlier in the day. He continued humming his tune, seemingly unaware that I was standing no more than six feet away.

"Nathan?" My voice cracked as I called his name.

Carrie's husband continued to rock and hum. I racked my brain for something that would capture his attention.

"Allie and Riley are waiting for you to tuck them in." It was a lie, but any father in their right mind would immediately react to their children wanting them.

But Nathan didn't.

That isn't Nathan. The words drifted through my mind unexpectedly, making me gasp in surprise. Although I couldn't see his face, I knew for a fact this man *was* Nathan. I already had searched the house from top to bottom. Only the four family members resided here. Who else could it be?

Then I had a chilling realization. It was Nathan on the outside. . .but maybe someone else was on the *inside.* Instantly, I knew what to say next. I took a deep, shaky breath as I prepared to speak the Latin exorcism prayer that I'd memorized a few months prior.

"Exorcizámos te, ómnis immúnde spiritus—"

My words were barely above a whisper, but Nathan's head whipped around in response and his black eyes bore into mine. I stumbled backward, heart pounding heavily as fear pulsed through me.

A sarcastic grin spread across his chiseled face. In a voice that was much deeper and raspier than his own, he said, "Sorry, Princess. That's not going to work on me."

"*Ómnis satanic potéstas*," I continued, ignoring him. Although I knew very little about demons, I was aware of the little tricks they liked to play to get out of being exorcised.

My words came to a halt as Nathan's mouth opened wide — so wide that I feared his skin would tear. Silence filled the room around us. Then suddenly Nathan let out a demonic roar that vibrated the air around me and sent his putrid breath flying in my direction.

I damn near dropped my phone as I spun around and bolted for the stairs, gagging and tripping over my own feet along the way. As soon as I reached the top, I slammed the door shut and locked it. Pushing past Carrie, I rushed into the living room and shoved my belongings into the two duffel bags I'd brought with me.

"What happened?" Carrie demanded, trailing me.

"He's possessed!" I shouted. I instantly felt bad for yelling at her, but fear and adrenaline made it difficult for me to be calm.

"What!" Her eyes widened in disbelief.

"Carrie, listen to me." I kept my eyes locked on hers, trying to convey the urgency through them. "You need to grab your kids and get out of here."

"But they're sleeping. . ."

"Now!"

Tears were streaming down her face, her bottom lip trembling. Pushing her dark brown bangs to the side, she ran a shaky hand across her forehead. "But he's my husband. I can't leave him behind."

"You have to," I stated firmly. "A demon is possessing his body, Carrie." I clenched and unclenched my jaw as my voice turned cold. "I'm sorry, but that's not your husband anymore."

"No!" she screamed in denial.

Without another word, I flung both duffel bags over my shoulder and made a beeline for the front door. I stepped out into the cool night. A thin layer of clouds covered the full moon, making the night appear even more sinister. I rushed toward my Jeep, which was parked at the end of the driveway.

"Ava!" Carrie's frightened voice came from behind me. "Please don't go. We need you!"

I swallowed the lump in my throat as I turned to tell her the truth. "I can't help you. I-I'm sorry," I stammered as tears threatened to spill out. "I've never been up against a demon before. I'm not good enough to deal with this on my own!"

"So you're just leaving us alone to *die*?" Her voice was thick with anger and a sense of betrayal.

Guilt slammed into me. I'd never walked out on a case before. But my life had never been in danger like this before either. Did choosing my life over theirs make me a coward? Probably. Perhaps a coward like me shouldn't be a paranormal investigator after all...

"Look, I have to get out of here and so should you." Before she could protest, I rambled on. "I'll find a local priest or someone who's better fit for exorcisms, but for now you *have* to leave."

I threw my bags in the Jeep and opened the driver's-side door.

"Ava, please," Carrie begged.

"I'm sorry," I muttered softly before climbing in and driving away.

I spared one last glance into the rearview mirror. Carrie was still standing at the end of the driveway, waving me down. My heart ached at the sight. It took only a second for me to realize I could no longer see the house because it was now shrouded by smoke as dark as the night sky.

I slammed the brakes and threw the Jeep into park. I jumped out and began to run back to the house, but came to a dead stop when a snake-like tendril reached out from the smoke toward Carrie. My mouth opened to tell her to run, but a bloodcurdling scream came out instead as the tendril wrapped around her body and yanked her backward into the smoky darkness.

CHAPTER TWO

"Ava!" I could barely hear the panicked voice calling for me above my own screaming.

"Ava, wake up!" the voice called again.

I sat bolt upright in bed, heart pounding and gasping for air. Every inch of my body was drenched in sweat.

"Austin!" I cried as I flung myself into my boyfriend's open arms.

"Shh," he soothed as he rubbed circles on my back. "It's okay, babe. It was just another nightmare."

Pressing my face against his cool neck, I mumbled, "No. It was the *same* nightmare."

"I had a feeling it was," he said, sighing. Gently, he untangled himself from me. His eyebrows drew together in concern as he gave me a onceover. "All that happened three years ago. . ."

"Except the ending with the weird smoke," I pointed out, as if he didn't already know. Sheesh, the man had heard the story so many times that he could recount the details as clearly as if he'd been there himself.

"Well, yeah. But why are you just now getting nightmares from it?"

I shrugged and looked down at my lap. If I knew the answer to that, I would've done something about it by now. Having the same nightmare for two weeks was more than enough. Maybe PTSD had finally caught up to me. Maybe I needed to see a shrink and get medicated. Or maybe. . .

"Maybe they're not really nightmares." The words I was thinking slipped out of my mouth without notice.

"Huh?" Austin's face was a huge question mark. "What do you mean?"

"I-I don't know," I stammered, just as confused by my own words. My forehead wrinkled thoughtfully as I stared off into the distance.

Austin wrapped my hands in his. "Tell me what you're thinking."

My gaze drifted back to him. A thin white T-shirt hung loose on his torso, barely concealing the delicious muscles underneath. The pillow had already tousled his blond hair in the short time we had been asleep. His gorgeous blue eyes locked onto mine. I could see the concern in them, but past that I also saw trust, loyalty, and love. Always love.

We had met nearly five years ago when we were both called to a case in Oklahoma City. After secretly crushing on each other for a long time, the truth surfaced during our case at The Foster House over a year ago and we have been together ever since.

Since day one of him being in my life, I'd found myself able to confide in him without fear of judgment. No matter how crazy I sounded, he never made me feel it once. There was no reason to hold back my thoughts now.

I shifted slightly on the bed. "What if it's something *more* than a nightmare? Like a premonition."

"Premonitions forewarn you about something. You can't be forewarned about an event from the past."

"Okay." I drew out the word. "An omen then?"

"That would be more likely." When I remained silent, Austin continued. "I don't know what it would be indicating though."

"Me neither," I admitted quietly as I lowered my gaze.

I chewed my bottom lip as I thought. Austin watched me carefully. One of the many things I've always loved about him is that he never tries to rush me.

I allowed myself to think back to that terrible night three years ago. Running out on Carrie and her family was the biggest mistake I'd ever made. Everyone in the house lost their lives because of me — including Carrie's unborn child. Authorities say her husband, Nathan, had gone insane and killed the family before killing himself. Only I know differently — a demon made him do it.

Ever since then, I'd searched for the opportunity to right my wrongs. Now I purposely seek out cases that might involve possession. Not many have come my way, and most turn out to be false alarms. Austin and I have taken on a handful of them together over the past year and a half — ever since we combined our paranormal investigation businesses after word of our success at The Foster House spread. We have an agreement that I do the dirty work of performing exorcisms while he stands by as backup. Damning every demon back to the deepest, darkest depths of hell is my way of making up for my past mistake.

And boy, do I love it! Adrenaline, relief, and euphoria fill me every time I complete an exorcism; officially ridding the world of the dark entity while saving an innocent life — or multiple lives in some cases. No amount of lives I save will bring the Johnson family back and no amount of demons I damn to hell will get rid of the one at fault, but. . .

Realization slammed into me, bringing my thoughts to a halt. "I've got it!"

Austin jerked at my sudden outburst. "Got what?"

"I didn't exorcise the demon. When the family died, it was left behind — lingering around, waiting for someone new to torment and feast on."

"It would've moved on by now."

"Not if something is holding it there," I countered.

"I'm sure other people have lived there since then."

I shook my head wildly, causing my hair to whip me in the face. "No! I kept tabs on the house after it was put on the market. Nobody ever moved in." Austin cocked an eyebrow at me, clearly questioning my sanity. "I stopped checking a few months ago." His expression didn't change. "Hey! Stop looking at me like I'm a crazy person."

He chuckled and leaned in to kiss my forehead. "You're *my* crazy person, though."

Even though we'd been dating for a year and a half now, he still managed to make me blush with his cheeseball lines. Yes, it's embarrassing, but I wouldn't have it any other way.

Austin's face turned serious again as he asked, "What do you think we should do?"

"We should check out the house."

"Agreed." He lay back down and pulled the blankets over himself. "I'll do whatever it takes to stop these nightmares from haunting you."

I lay down beside him, resting my head on his chest. "I love you, Austin."

"I love you too."

Curled up in the safety of my lover's arms, I quickly drifted off into a peaceful sleep.

* * *

Edmond, Oklahoma, is a little over an hour and a half from our home in Broken Arrow. By the time we arrived, it was a little after noon. We swung by a Whataburger drive-through before navigating our way to the Johnson family's old home.

Austin parked his Lexus along the sidewalk across from the house. I leaned forward in my seat, looking past him. The Victorian-style house stood out from the more modern homes on Cherry Street. White trim lined the front windows, making the slate blue siding pop. The front porch was almost the entire width of the house and was decorated with new-looking patio furniture and windchimes that swayed in the gentle breeze. Large columns supported the roof overhead while a paved driveway led up to a two-car garage that stood toward the back side of the property.

"Someone definitely lives here." When I realized my nightmares may have been an omen after all, my stomach tightened.

"It doesn't look like anyone's home, though," Austin said, noticing the empty driveway.

I looked at the dashboard clock. It was just after one o'clock on a Tuesday. Whoever lived there was probably at work or school.

"Let's hang out here for a bit," I suggested. "They're bound to come home eventually."

Austin agreed and grabbed the bag of food from my lap. He pulled out his portion — two fully loaded burgers and some fries — before passing it back to me. I had been starving since we left home, but nerves chased my appetite away. I put the bag on the floorboard and pulled out my cell phone. Playing games usually made the time pass by faster.

I was so absorbed in my game of Solitaire that I damn near had a heart attack when a Styx song suddenly blasted through the car speakers. I glared at Austin as he took a sip of Coke. He smiled and did a little toast in my direction before biting into his second burger. I rolled my eyes and shook my head.

"What?" he asked around a mouthful of burger.

"This must be what it's like to date Dean Winchester," I mused.

"So dating me is a dream come true then." He flashed me his adorable cocky grin.

I stuck my tongue out at him playfully before returning to my game. We remained parked for about an hour before deciding to drive around town — concerned the neighbors would make a fuss over us loitering. Around four o'clock, we returned to the house.

"Where the hell are they?" I groaned when I saw the empty driveway.

Austin shrugged. "Maybe they're on vacation or just getting off work. . .Wait," he said, looking through the sideview mirror. "A car is coming."

Crossing my fingers, I hoped and prayed the approaching vehicle was the family we'd waited all afternoon for. When the burgundy minivan turned into the driveway, I had to resist the urge to do a little happy dance.

A tall, burly, dark-haired man who appeared to be in his late thirties climbed out of the driver's seat. Judging by his dirty clothes and heavy-duty work boots, I gathered he was just getting off work — perhaps at a construction site or a factory. He slid the back door open and reached inside. When he emerged, he was holding a little boy with bright blond hair. He shut the door and carried the child toward the house.

Meanwhile, on the passenger side, a woman with sandy-blonde hair and wearing casual clothes appeared to be scolding the teenage version of herself. Seriously, the only difference between the two was the obvious age gap, and the teen had dark brown hair with highlights. It seemed the two finally came to an agreement and loaded bags of groceries on their arms before following the other two into the house.

After they were all inside, I turned to Austin. "Should we get out and greet them?"

His eyes narrowed. "And what exactly do you plan on saying?"

I chewed my bottom lip. What would I say? *Hey, are there any demons living here rent free? Because I kind of ran away from one a few years ago, which caused an entire family to die and lately I've been having nightmares that may hint at it being back.* Yeah, right. That would *not* end well.

"Don't worry. I'll figure something out," I said, waving a hand dismissively.

"Just remember, I'm not *really* Dean, so fake IDs can't be involved in whatever white lie you have brewing in that pretty little head of yours."

"No, really?" I replied, making him laugh.

We remained in the car a few more minutes, making sure the family was settled in for the evening and allowing me time to come up with a half-decent lie. Finally, we got out of the car and walked toward the house. Once we were on the porch, I held my breath and rang the doorbell.

A few seconds later the door swung open, and the older woman appeared, now wearing a gray T-shirt and baggy sweatpants. Her hair was pulled back into a messy bun. She smiled sweetly at us.

"Can I help you?"

"Oh, um, sorry. I didn't realize someone else lived here," I replied sheepishly. "I used to babysit for a family here, but I lost touch when I moved away. Since I was in town for a visit, I thought I'd drop by to see them."

"You don't by any chance know Carrie and Nathan Johnson, do you?" Austin asked her, joining in my lie.

She gave us an apologetic look. "I'm sorry, I don't. The house was on the market for quite a while before my husband and I bought it. We never had the chance to meet the previous owners."

"Oh, I see." I faked disappointment.

"How old are the kids? If they're still in the area, my daughter might know them."

I thought for a moment. "They'd be around six years old now. Twin girls, Allie and Riley."

"Oh, my daughter wouldn't know them then. She's a senior in high school." The woman tilted her head slightly. "How long ago did you babysit them?"

"Three years ago."

Her brows shot up to her hairline. "Wow! So you babysat twin toddlers on your own?" When I nodded, she shook her head and laughed. "That must have been a handful."

I smiled. "It sure was."

"Well, we should get going," Austin said, lightly touching my arm.

"Yeah, you're right," I told him. Then I turned to the woman. "It was nice to meet you. Sorry for bothering you."

As Austin and I began walking away, the woman called after us. "Hang on!" We turned around to face her. "Would you two like to stay for dinner?" I opened my mouth to kindly reject her offer, but she continued. "You came out here hoping to see old friends. It's the least I can do."

I glanced at Austin, who shrugged in response. Turning back to the woman, I said, "I don't know. . ."

"We're having biscuits and gravy with hot apple pie for dessert."

"Pie?" Austin repeated excitedly. The woman nodded and Austin stepped forward, holding his hand out to her. "Hi, I'm Austin Reed and this is Ava Moore. We'd be delighted to stay for dinner."

"I'm Melissa Lloyd." She laughed as she stepped aside and gestured inside the house. "Come on in."

CHAPTER THREE

An eerie feeling settled over me as I stepped into the house. Was it due to a big bad demon lingering around, or was it because of the tragic memories haunting me? I took a quick glance at Austin, who appeared relaxed and unbothered, as if everything were normal here. *I guess it's just me.*

"Follow me," Melissa said.

The wooden floorboards creaked occasionally as we followed her toward the back of the house where I recalled the kitchen and dining room being. Antique sconces lit our path. The walls were a mixture of dark wood paneling and floral wallpaper. As we passed the cellar door, a shiver ran through me. It was closed, just as I had left it three years ago.

"How long have you lived here?" Austin asked.

"Only about a month."

Austin and I exchanged glances. My nightmares had started two weeks ago. The theory of them being an omen was becoming more and more likely. Melissa seemed happy, though; I sensed no fear or apprehension from her. Perhaps we got here just in time. *Now how do we get them out of here before anything bad happens?*

"We have some guests for dinner," Melissa announced as we stepped into the kitchen.

The kitchen was large with beautiful cherrywood cabinets and black marble countertops. A matching island stood near the center of the room. The stainless-steel appliances looked brand new. Three doorways led into the kitchen: the one we had come through, one that led to the dining room, and another leading into a large room the Johnson's had used as a study.

A man, who was facing the stove when we entered, spun around. He was hardly recognizable now that he was sporting a clean T-shirt that showed off his overly large muscles and basketball shorts rather than his dirty work gear. Judging by his damp hair, it was safe to assume he'd already showered off the dirt and grime in the short time he'd been home. Melissa pranced over to him and looped one arm through his.

"This is my husband, Derek." She looked at him and gestured toward us with one hand. "And this is Austin and Ava. They came here looking for the family that used to live here."

When Melissa spoke my name, a strange look flitted through Derek's eyes. Almost like he recognized me. Austin and I are sort of well-known in the paranormal investigation world through our videos on YouTube as well as the multitude of cases we have taken on over the years that put our faces in newspapers and on social media pages. Derek could be a fan wondering why we're here. But something about the way he looked at me had my stomach twisting. As if sensing my discomfort, Austin stepped closer to me, wrapping a protective arm around my waist.

Derek turned his attention to Austin and smiled. "It's nice to meet you."

"You too," Austin replied. I hoped I was the only one that noticed his standoffish tone.

Derek looked at Melissa. "Food's almost ready."

"I'll get the kids," she said, then left the room.

Derek turned around to face the stove again, leaving Austin and me standing around awkwardly. Thankfully, Melissa returned within a couple of minutes carrying the little boy. His big brown eyes shone brightly as he looked at Austin and me.

"This is Brayden," she told us.

"Hi, Brayden." I smiled at him.

A grin spread across his little face. "Hi!"

"Oh, my goodness. He's so cute!" I gushed as I stepped closer to touch his chubby little arm. "How old is he?"

"Eighteen months." Brayden reached out to me with his two tiny arms. Melissa chuckled. "I guess Bray doesn't want Mama today. Do you want to hold him?"

"Sure!" I replied excitedly. I absolutely love kids but never have the chance to be around them much.

Once I got Brayden adjusted on my hip, he rested his little blond head on my shoulder. My heart instantly melted. I walked back to Austin, who smiled in adoration.

"Do you think they'd let me keep him?" I whispered.

"I don't think so," he whispered back. Then he flashed me that adorable cocky grin of his. "But if you really want one. . ."

I pointed a finger at him and gave a warning glare. "Don't tempt me."

"Where's Jessica?" Derek asked.

"I'm here." The teenager poked her head in through the doorway leading to the dining room. "Mom asked me to set the table."

"Jess, these are our guests, Ava and Austin," Melissa told her daughter.

The young girl gave me a onceover and a knowing smile formed on her face. She turned her eyes to Austin, and her smile turned flirtatious. I allowed her little teenage eyes to linger on my man for two seconds longer than necessary before I stepped protectively in front of him, almost completely blocking her view.

"Hi, Jessica." I flashed her my friendliest smile. "It's nice to meet you."

"You too. And you can call me Jess." She flipped her wavy dark brown hair over her shoulder and returned to the dining room.

"You're more than welcome to go on in and sit down if you'd like," Melissa told Austin and me as she gestured toward the dining room.

When we entered the room, I was half expecting to see the long, glass table the Johnson family had owned — you know, the kind that belongs in the dining hall of a royal palace — but was relieved to see a much smaller wooden table instead. An old cabinet filled with fancy china was centered along one wall. I never understood why people owned such expensive dishes that were rarely touched, if ever.

"I'll take Bray," Jess said, reaching out to claim her brother. She nodded toward two chairs. "You two can sit over there. Do you want anything to drink? We have milk, water, tea, apple juice, caffeine-free Coke, and enough beer to call our kitchen a bar."

"*Caffeine-free* Coke?" I wrinkled my nose in disgust.

"That's how I feel too. Mom thinks caffeine is too addictive for her family to consume. Whatever," she scoffed, rolling her eyes.

I smiled. "Well, I'll just have some tea then. Thanks."

"Tea here too, please," Austin said.

Jess put Brayden in his booster seat then disappeared into the kitchen. As soon as she was out of earshot, Austin turned to me.

"What are you thinking?"

"I'm thinking Jess has the hots for you," I muttered.

"Can you blame her?" He smirked.

I rolled my eyes and playfully smacked his arm. "Everything feels. . .off," I admitted, turning serious again. "I don't know if something is actually happening here or if I'm imagining things."

Austin nodded in understanding. "The family seems fairly normal — happy even. Maybe the you-know-what isn't here after all."

"Yeah maybe. . ."

Our conversation came to an end when Jess returned with her parents trailing, each with their hands full of food and drinks. Melissa and Derek sat the pile of steaming hot biscuits and a pot of gravy in the center of the table while Jess passed out the drinks. When she sat a glass of dark-brown carbonated liquid in front of me, I gave her a confused look.

"Just drink it," she whispered, then took a seat across the table from me.

Hesitantly, I put the glass up to my mouth. When the tingly sweetness of sugar-loaded, fully caffeinated Coke hit my tongue, I smiled with pleasure. My questioning eyes locked onto Jess and she winked. *Teenagers sure are sneaky.*

Once everyone was seated, we piled our plates with delicious food.

"Have you guys always lived in Edmond?" I asked casually.

"No," Melissa replied. "We moved here from Phoenix."

"Any particular reason? If you don't mind me asking."

"I don't mind at all!" She smiled warmly at me. "Derek was offered a big promotion if we were willing to relocate."

I turned to Derek. "Congratulations!"

"What kind of work do you do?" Austin asked him.

"Thank you." Derek nodded in my direction before answering Austin. "I'm a manager for Day Build Construction."

"That's cool. My dad works in construction too."

Ignoring Austin's friendly attempt at making a connection, Derek looked at me. "What do you do for a living?"

"Oh, um, I, uh, work in retail." Usually, I'm better prepared with fake answers, but Derek's strange interest in me and his slightly intimidating stare threw me off guard.

"What about you, Austin?" Jess's tone sounded curious, but the way her eyes focused everywhere on his body except his face made it obvious that his career choice was the last thing she was curious about.

Austin shifted uncomfortably under her watchful eyes. "I'm a personal trainer."

Yeah, like *that* information was going to make Jess back off. I closed my eyes as I fought against the urge to smack him upside the head.

"Mm-hmm." Jess looked between the two of us intently. Could she tell we were lying?

"Do you work as well, Melissa?" I asked, steering the conversation away from Austin and me.

"Yes. I work at a daycare near the Oklahoma City Zoo."

"The daycare *is* a zoo," Jess joked, making us all laugh.

"So, how are you liking your new school?" I asked Jess once the laughter died down.

She shrugged. "It's okay, I guess. Being the new girl in senior year isn't easy, though."

"I imagine it's difficult," I said sympathetically. "Any plans for college?"

Jess nodded. "I want to be a pediatric nurse."

"That's awesome!"

"Playing an important role in the lives of children, just like her mom," Melissa said, grinning proudly at her daughter.

Derek scoffed. "We can't afford that."

"Who asked *you* to pay for it?" Jess snapped as she glared at her dad, who continued to eat his food without another word.

We spent the remainder of the meal getting to know each other. Melissa and I bonded over our love for travel. She shared some of her favorite memories from her time in Europe during a study-abroad program in college. That is also where her and Derek's beautiful love story began. Austin had gone to Europe with his family long before I met him, so he was able to relate to some of Melissa's stories.

Jess's hobbies mainly consisted of binge watching reality TV shows and reading. I instantly connected with her on the latter of the two, and learned we had some favorite authors in common, namely Stephen King and James Patterson. Austin isn't much of a reader, so it was nice to have someone to discuss books with for a change.

Once everyone had finished eating the main course, Melissa stepped into the kitchen to grab the pie for dessert. When she passed Austin the first slice, his face lit up like a kid who'd been given a lifetime supply of candy. I smiled at the childish excitement radiating from him.

He shoved the first bite into his mouth and moaned. "Mmmm. So good."

"Did you make this yourself?" I asked Melissa, then took a bite. It was one of the best apple pies I'd ever tasted.

Derek burst out in humorless laughter. "That woman can't cook worth shit."

Melissa's eyes filled with tears. It was obvious his rude remark hurt her feelings. *What an ass.*

"Dad made the pie," Jess said softly, laying a comforting hand on her mother's arm.

We all finished our pie in silence. Derek left the room without another word. Like a true gentleman, Austin began clearing the table without being asked. Melissa helped him while Jess and I worked together to clean up the mess Brayden had made.

"We should probably head home now," Austin said to me once everything was cleaned up.

"Yeah, it's getting late," I agreed.

"Thanks for the delicious meal, Melissa," Austin said.

"You're welcome." She smiled warmly. "I'm sorry about my husband's rude behavior earlier. This new job has been stressing him out a lot."

Austin nodded. "Managing a company isn't easy."

"Let me walk you out."

As we approached the front door, Derek stepped out from the living room. "Leaving already?"

"Yes, sir," Austin replied.

"Sorry for intruding on your evening," I told Melissa.

"Oh, it was no intrusion at all!" she assured me sweetly. "You're the first visitors we've had here. It was much needed."

"Feel free to drop in again sometime," Derek said. Although his words were friendly and inviting, his flat tone and intense stare made them sound like a challenge — almost like he was *daring* us to return.

"We might just take you up on that," I said evenly, staring right back at him.

As Austin and I stepped outside, Melissa called out, "Be safe!"

"You too," Austin told her as he pulled the door shut behind us.

I was lost in my own thoughts as we walked toward the Lexus. When Nathan was possessed, Carrie was absolutely terrified of him. There was no happiness and laughter in the home — only fear and anger. I didn't sense the same thing with this family. Sure, Derek was a little weird and a bit of an asshole, but I'd met worse.

Austin unlocked the car doors. Before we could climb inside, a girl's voice sounded from across the street.

"Guys, wait!" Jess was running barefoot down the driveway. By the time she made it to us, she was out of breath. Clearly, she was no star athlete. "I have to tell you something. . .or ask you. . .or, I don't know."

"What is it?" I asked.

She crossed her arms over her chest and chewed her bottom lip nervously. Her eyes darted back and forth between Austin and me.

"You can tell us anything," I assured her.

"I, um, I know you're paranormal investigators."

"How do you know that?" Austin asked.

"I heard about you guys sometime last year and binge watched your YouTube videos," she admitted sheepishly. "It was after that one big case you did in Arkansas."

"The Foster House," I said.

"Yeah, that." She inhaled deeply. When she spoke again, her words flowed out in one breath. "Look, I don't have money to pay you guys, and maybe it's not even something you can help with, but my family is in danger."

"Danger?" I repeated.

Austin looked around like he was ready to fight whatever it was. "What kind of danger?"

"I-I don't really know, but something is causing trouble in our house." Jess's brown eyes glistened with unshed tears. Her bottom lip quivered as she looked Austin squarely in the eyes. "And I'm afraid if it isn't stopped, my family is going to die."

CHAPTER FOUR

Her words shouldn't have come as a shock to me. After all, I'd thought the nightmares were a sign that another family was in danger, which was what brought us here now. But if I was prepared for this, why was my heart pounding to hard? And why were my legs like jelly? I wanted to flee this town and never look back — or at least have a total mental breakdown. It took every ounce of energy to maintain my composure.

I felt Austin's eyes on me, studying me, but I kept mine locked on Jess. As always, Austin could sense what I was feeling. He moved closer and wrapped a comforting arm around my waist.

"Why do you think your family will die, Jess?" Austin asked.

"I-it's a long story." She glanced nervously at the house behind her then lowered her voice. "I don't think we should talk here, though."

She was right. Not only were her parents likely to question us loitering on the side of the road, but also, if the demon were around, it could hear everything — and that would be *very* bad. The very thought of what could happen sent a chill throughout my body.

"Maybe we could meet up with you somewhere," I suggested.

"I have an hour lunch break at school," she said. "Seniors are allowed to leave the property. Could we do it tomorrow?"

"Absolutely," I said. "Where should we meet you?"

Jess nibbled on her fingernails as she thought. "Fairwood Park is just down the street from my school. How about there?"

"Fairwood Park it is," I agreed.

"Lunch starts at eleven. It'll only take a couple of minutes to walk there. I'll meet you at the entrance."

"We'll be there," I assured her. "See you tomorrow."

Before we parted ways, Austin placed a comforting hand on her shoulder. "It'll be okay, Jess."

The girl practically melted under his touch and her face beamed bright red. I rolled my eyes as I made my way to the passenger side of the car. By the time I got in, Austin was already sitting behind the wheel and Jess was halfway up the driveway.

"She knows we're together, right?" Austin joked.

"She'd better or else I might sacrifice her to the demon myself," I grumbled while I fumbled with my seat belt.

He grinned teasingly. "Jealous?"

"Please," I scoffed. "I don't get jealous."

"Good. Because you're the only girl for me. *Always*."

He leaned over and gently pressed his lips to mine. The warmth and love wrapped up in that one kiss was enough to wipe all thoughts from my mind. Sadly, it ended too soon and I began thinking about the horrific things Jess could possibly tell us tomorrow.

The entire way home, I stared silently out the window. The fall foliage whirred by in a blur of red, orange, and brown, but I could not get myself to admire its beauty during such a dark time. Before long, Austin was turning the car into our driveway.

Inside, I kicked off my shoes and turned to him. "What's the plan now?"

"I guess we should pack our bags and prepare to be gone for at least a couple of days."

"What did we miss?" I asked, my voice quavering. "They seemed fine!"

"I don't know." Austin sighed as he ran a hand through his blond hair, causing it to stick up in the front.

Finally, the dam inside me broke and tears flowed down my face. "This is all my fault!"

"Babe, no." Austin quickly stepped forward and wrapped me in his strong arms. "This isn't your fault."

"If I hadn't run away. . ."

His arms tightened around me as he stroked my hair with one hand. "Stop blaming yourself. Besides, we don't know if Jess's family is going through the same thing or not."

"What if they are, though?" I sobbed. "What if I'm still just the coward who runs away and they—"

He cut me off firmly. "That won't happen." He held me at arm's length and wiped the tears from my face. "You're way more experienced now than you were three years ago. You've even taken on demons since then. Most importantly, you have *me* this time. I won't let anything hurt you or that family."

"I wish I'd had you with me the first time," I said quietly.

"I would've been there in a heartbeat if I hadn't been all the way in Boston. I'm sorry."

"Don't apologize. You were on a case. I wouldn't have expected you to drop everything for me anyway."

He rested his hands on my hips, pressing his forehead against mine. "Either way, I'll be there this time, and we'll get rid of whatever is in that house once and for all. I promise. In the meantime, let's hear what Jess has to say tomorrow and go from there, okay?"

The way his rock hard body was pressed against mine with his lips mere inches away had my pulse quickening. He still had the same irresistible, breathtaking effect on me as day one.

"Okay," I replied breathlessly. "Let's go pack."

"Actually, I have a better idea." He grinned mischievously as his lips moved closer to mine and his arms wrapped tightly around my waist.

"Mmm. I like this idea so far." I tilted my head up slightly.

The moment our lips met, every bit of fear and worry within me turned into raw passion. A small moan escaped me as I wrapped my arms around Austin's neck, pulling him as close as possible. My fingers trailed upward to play with his hair. Once I tugged gently on it, it was game over. His hands slid down to the back of my thighs, and then he hoisted me into the air. Wrapping my legs around his waist, I held on as he carried me into the bedroom.

And that's the story of how I became relaxed enough to sleep that night. What, did you really think I was going to give you all the dirty details?

CHAPTER FIVE

At five past eleven, Austin and I saw Jess strolling up the sidewalk leading to Fairwood Park. She spotted us getting out of the Lexus and jogged the rest of the way to us.

"Hey, guys," she greeted us. "Glad you could make it."

"Likewise," Austin said. "Where should we go to talk?"

There were several people walking along the trail that circled the perimeter of the park. A couple of kids were having a blast on the playground equipment while their parents sat around with their eyes glued to their cell phones.

Jess glanced around before pointing to an empty picnic table near a cluster of oak trees halfway across the park. "That looks like a good spot."

Once we were all seated around the table, Austin pulled out his trusty voice recorder. Gesturing toward it, he asked Jess, "Do you mind?"

"Not at all," she replied.

He pressed the "record" button and began. "Can you tell us why you feel your family is in danger?"

Jess clasped her hands together on the table and inhaled deeply. "We used to be one big happy family until we moved here. Dad was always helping out around the house and spent a lot of quality time with us. He never yelled, laid a hand on anyone, or made us feel unloved or unwanted in any way."

"That's not the case now?" I asked.

Jess shook her head sadly. "He's so angry all the time now. Quality time with Bray and me has become a thing of the past." She paused to scoff. "What little time we do get with him usually ends in an argument."

"The way he was toward you and your mom yesterday," Austin started. "Is that his normal behavior?"

"It's his *new* normal. He wasn't like that in Phoenix."

"Your mom told us he's been stressed from working so much," I said. "Do you think maybe that's the reason he's changed?"

"At first I believed that." Tears pooled in her eyes. "A few days ago, I was upstairs in my room, and I heard a man yelling in a really deep, scary voice. I snuck downstairs to see what was going on. It was my dad. He was yelling at Mom." Her tears finally broke free and streamed down, dripping onto the wooden table top. "She was saying something, but I couldn't make it out. I could tell she was scared, though. Then out of nowhere he slapped her! Does that sound like *work stress* to you?"

"No," I replied quietly.

"Did you call anyone for help?" Austin asked.

"N-no," she spoke between sobs. "B-but the guy that hit her wasn't m-my dad."

"What do you mean?" I was more than a little confused. It was her dad, but it wasn't?

"I mean, it was him, but it wasn't *him*." She squinted and shook her head, appearing just as confused by her own words as I was. "Sorry, that probably makes no sense."

"That's okay," Austin assured her. "Did he look different?"

"Sort of, I guess. His body was tense and his eyes were dark, almost black." She shrugged. "Maybe that's just how he is when he gets mad, though. I've never seen him that angry before to know for sure."

I recalled how Nathan's eyes looked when I'd encountered him in the cellar — so black it almost looked like he had no eyes at all. His voice had been deep and scary too, like Jess had said Derek's was when he was yelling at Melissa.

"So when you said it *wasn't* your dad…" Austin started.

"I mean it wasn't the same guy I've known my whole life. My dad would never do something like that."

"When exactly did he start acting different?" I asked.

"Maybe a week or so after we moved here. He started off being easily irritated and distant. Over the last few days, his temper has gotten worse."

"Has anything else been happening aside from daddy dearest turning into a total jackass?" Austin inquired rather bluntly. I smacked his arm, giving him a stern look. He rolled his eyes and mumbled. "Sorry."

"It's okay. You're right to say that," Jess told him. She picked at her fingernails as she continued. "I've seen doors open and close on their own. Sometimes things will disappear and show up again in the strangest places. I swear I hear someone whispering my name at night, but no one's ever there. Even Bray has been acting a little strange lately."

I raised my brows in surprise. "How so?"

"Over the weekend we were playing in the living room. I was talking to him, but something caught his attention and he looked toward the couch. He smiled and waved like someone was there. . ."

"But there wasn't," I finished for her. Stories like that were common in this line of work. Kids tend to be naturally more aware of spiritual presences than adults.

Jess shook her head. "It was so weird."

"Clearly the situation with your dad scares you," I said. "But how do the other strange happenings make you feel?"

Her brows drew together as she thought deeply. "I was a little scared when things first started happening. Who wouldn't be? It's all been harmless little pranks, though." She cracked a slight smile. "Besides, if Bray wasn't scared of what he saw, why should I be?"

"When did those harmless little pranks start happening?" I asked.

"The day we moved in."

"So the danger you feel is really just your dad?" I clarified. Jess nodded in response.

Although no one else was around to overhear, Austin lowered his voice. "Is he the reason you think your family could die?"

"Yes," Jess whispered. She hesitated before adding, "He bought a gun on Monday."

Memories of the news reports on the Johnson family's death flashed through my mind. All of the victims — including Nathan — had died by gunshot wounds. Detectives had found a 9mm handgun on the ground next to Nathan's body, with his fingerprints all over it. That's what led them to believe he committed the murders before taking his own life.

"Welcome to Oklahoma," Austin joked half-heartedly. I threw him a *Would you shut up?* glare.

"We've never had a gun in our home," Jess stated somberly, ignoring Austin's effort of lightening the mood.

"You're afraid he's going to completely snap," I said. It wasn't a question, but Jess nodded in response anyway. Tears fell down her face once again. I moved to the other side of the picnic table and put an arm around her. "We won't let that happen."

Austin reached across the table and grabbed one of her hands. "Even if it's nothing paranormal, we won't let any of you get hurt."

"Thank you," she said softly.

I pulled my cell phone out to check the time. It was almost eleven forty-five. Jess would need to get back to school soon.

"All right, Austin and I need time to talk everything over. In the meantime, go back to school. I'll let you know what we come up with later."

Jess looked concerned. "You're not going to call the cops on my dad, are you?"

"Not unless we have to," I said.

I unlocked my phone and added her name and phone number to my contacts. Then I sent her a text so she'd know it was me when I called her later.

"We'll be in touch soon," I told her.

"Thanks again," she said. "I'll talk to you later."

"See ya," Austin said.

Austin and I remained at the park while we processed the new information. It was all so. . .conflicting.

"What do you think is going on?" I asked.

He blew out a mouthful of air and rubbed his face. "I don't even know. Some of it sounds like a fun little poltergeist."

"That's what Carrie Johnson thought too," I pointed out.

"Wasn't she afraid of it, though?"

He was right. Throughout the short time I'd been in touch with Carrie, she was scared of *everything* going on. The only thing Jess feared was her dad.

I sighed. "Maybe it really is a poltergeist this time and Derek is just an asshat who needs to learn how to manage his stress levels."

Austin nodded. "That's a possibility. We should still investigate just to be sure, though."

"Agreed."

"Come on." He stood up and held a hand out to me. "Let's get something to eat and find a hotel for the night."

Hand in hand we walked back to the car. I kept trying to convince myself it really was a poltergeist this time. Maybe if I'd allowed myself to accept the truth of the matter, I would have been much more prepared for what was to come.

CHAPTER SIX

I lay on the hotel room bed, staring at the ceiling. Jess would be out of school in a couple of hours, and I still hadn't decided what I should tell her. *Hey, Jess, so it sounds like a poltergeist, but it could also be the demon I ran from a while back. Oh, and it killed an entire family before, so your fears aren't totally irrational.* No way. I couldn't tell her anything that would freak her out and make her parents suspicious. Maybe I. . .

"Stop stressing," Austin said from the little desk across the room. His back was to me as he focused on his laptop screen.

Propping myself up on my elbows, I asked, "How did you—"

"I can feel it." He spun the chair around to face me. "We aren't going to tell Jess or her parents anything until we know for sure what's going on in that house."

"Then what am I supposed to tell her?"

He shrugged. "Just tell her the truth — that we need to investigate the house to find the answer."

"And how do we investigate the house without Melissa and Derek being suspicious?" I asked, wrinkling my forehead in confusion.

"I'm sure Jess is devious enough to figure something out." He turned to face his laptop again.

With a heavy sigh, I stood up and walked over to him. I draped an arm around his shoulders and bent over slightly to look at the screen.

"What are you so deeply invested in over here?"

"I'm digging up some history on the house."

"Anything useful so far?"

"It was built in 1901 and has been a hot spot for death ever since."

I furrowed my brow. "A hot spot for death? As in entire families being mysteriously murdered or just Grandma kicking the bucket at ninety years old?"

"That's what I'm trying to find out now." He clicked to another webpage and pointed to a list of dates and names. "This is the purchase history of the house. Strange that it's been put up for sale every few years, isn't it?"

"Very strange," I muttered.

Another webpage showed an old-fashioned death certificate. "This is the original homeowner, William Mason. He died in 1931."

I studied the document. My brows shot up when I read the cause of death. "He was stabbed?"

Austin nodded. "Multiple times by his nineteen-year-old son, James. The mom was killed too."

"What happened to James afterward?"

"That's where things get interesting. Within a few weeks, he became mysteriously wealthy, put the house up for sale, and fled the country — never to be heard from again."

"He wasn't arrested?" I asked in disbelief.

"He was, but at the trial they found him not guilty by reason of insanity due to the hardships his family had faced during the Great Depression."

"Sounds to me like someone offered him a lot of money in exchange for the lives of his parents." I lifted a single eyebrow. "Maybe he made a deal with the Devil."

Austin narrowed his eyes at me. "This isn't an episode of *Supernatural*."

I rolled my eyes. "It's just a theory."

"Have you ever known someone to make a deal like that outside of fictional movies and books?"

"Well, no," I admitted. "But that doesn't mean it isn't possible. Do you have a more logical explanation for it?"

"No." He sighed and rubbed the back of his neck. "But all these deaths taking place could explain the house being haunted in general. I'm sure some of their spirits are restless and still hanging around."

"That's true."

"I'll keep searching, though. There's bound to be more clues out there somewhere."

"Need any help?" I asked.

"How about I take the reins on the research part this time?" He tilted his head up to look at me. "You focus on calling Jess and using that sneaky little mind of yours to help her come up with a plan for getting us inside the house to investigate."

I smiled down at him. "Deal."

After giving him a quick peck on the cheek, I returned to the bed and flipped on the TV. A *Friends* marathon was happening. Between laughing at Chandler's jokes and gasping for the millionth time at Ross's inability to say the correct name at the altar, I finally managed to clear my mind and relax.

Before I knew it, Jess was texting me to say she was walking home from school and had time to talk. I hit the "call" button and turned on the speakerphone.

Jess answered on the first ring. "What's the verdict?"

"We believe there *is* something in your house," I told her.

"Good or bad?" she asked, lowering her voice.

"We're not really sure," I admitted. "We have our suspicions, but we need to investigate the house to know for sure."

Jess sighed into the phone. "That won't be easy, you know."

"Your parents *did* offer for us to come back sometime," I reminded her.

"True, but they don't believe in anything paranormal." She paused to scoff. "They'd think we were all totally insane and probably try to lock us up somewhere if they found out why you were *really* here."

A headache was quickly developing from overthinking and stressing so much. I looked at Austin, hoping he'd have some suggestions, but he only shrugged. Well, hell.

"I have an idea!" Jess practically shouted, breaking the silence.

"Go on," I urged.

"I could tell my parents that I have a report due that involves interviewing someone of interest to me," she explained. "They won't suspect a thing!"

"Um, what if they ask you why *we*, of all people, are interesting enough to interview?" I asked.

"I'll tell them I recognized you from some videos online. They won't care enough to ask for any details past that."

"I guess that's a plan to get us in there." Austin's tone showed slight doubt. "That still doesn't give us the freedom to investigate, though."

"Let me finish, moron," Jess snapped.

Austin looked mildly offended, causing a bubble of laughter to escape my mouth. I quickly covered it with a cough.

"Go on," he told Jess flatly.

"My parents will be gone at work all day tomorrow. I'll skip school to let you roam around the house."

"Then why bother mentioning a fake interview if they won't even be around?" I asked.

I could practically hear her eyes rolling through the phone. "Because you *will* find something in the house and need an excuse to be around after they get home."

"Huh," I mused.

"Told you she'd be devious enough to figure something out," Austin said, smiling at me. "Nice work, Jess."

"Thanks," she replied sheepishly. I rolled my eyes at her infatuation with *my* boyfriend.

"What time do your parents go to work?" Austin asked.

"They leave around seven."

"Text us when they're gone. We'll be up and ready to go," he told her. "We're staying at a Holiday Inn here in Edmond. If you need anything before morning, let us know."

"Okay, I will," Jess said. "See you tomorrow."

Once the call ended, Austin continued researching while I turned my attention back to *Friends*. I managed to watch two more episodes in complete silence before Austin interrupted.

"Almost everyone who has lived in the house has died," he stated. "Death certificates and news reports show several different causes: homicide, suicide, and even some 'health complications'." He put air quotes around the last one. "There have been a couple of rare instances where families have fled the house in fear, which ultimately saved their lives."

"What's the death toll?"

"Twenty-three including the Johnson family. Twelve separate incidents."

"Holy shit," I gasped.

"Urban legends sprouted up in the late 1900s that hinted at supernatural forces being the cause for the deaths. The house was left empty for several years because of it," he explained. "Eventually the legends died out, but the place wasn't fit to sell anymore. An anonymous donation was received to repair it. As it's one of the oldest homes in the area, they didn't want to see it tore down."

I crossed my arms and narrowed my eyes. "So, despite the home's dark history, the state or whoever had ownership still chose to *sell* it?"

"And guess who the lucky buyers were?" he said humorlessly.

My heart dropped and my voice came out barely above a whisper. "The Johnson's."

Austin pressed his lips together and nodded. "I'm surprised it sold at all."

"It was the perfect size for their growing family, and the price was too good to be true," I recalled what Carrie had once told me. Swallowing past the lump in my throat, I continued. "They weren't from around here to know the legends or history of the house. They didn't know what they were getting themselves into."

Austin grabbed my hand, intertwining our fingers together. "Hopefully this case and everything we learn from it will finally give you the closure you need."

I nodded. "So it's obvious that a demon or some dark entity has killed all these people in the past, but has anything pointed to *why* it's there to begin with?"

"Not that I've found so far, but I still have plenty of time to search before tomorrow morning. We'll figure this out," he assured me. "In the meantime, you need to prepare yourself."

I smirked. "I'm always prepared to kick some paranormal ass."

His expression was serious as his eyes met mine. "This isn't our usual ass-kicking case. You need to prepare yourself for all hell to break loose."

"Bring it on!"

On the outside, I was all confidence and cockiness. But on the inside, I was ready to hightail it back home like the coward I still was.

CHAPTER SEVEN

Sleep didn't come easily for Austin and me. We were awake and ready to go before the clock even turned six. Knowing we still had a good hour or more, we grabbed some breakfast in the hotel lobby. At a quarter past seven, my phone chimed with a text from Jess. The house was officially empty — with the exception of herself and whatever spooks were lurking around.

"It's show time," I told Austin.

He flung the backpack that held our paranormal investigation equipment over his shoulder. Together we left the hotel. The bright morning sun was still on the rise, painting the sky with gorgeous shades of yellow, orange, and red.

No lights appeared to be on inside the house and the driveway was empty. Jess was nowhere to be seen. Austin raised his fist to knock, but just then the door swung open.

"Hey," Jess greeted us.

"Hey." I peered around her into the dark house. "Why are the lights out?"

She shrugged. "I tried to make it seem like nobody was home until the nosey couple next door left." She stepped to the side for Austin and me to enter. "I didn't want them to tell my parents I skipped school."

"Smart." I nodded in approval.

"Alright." Austin clapped his hands together. "Let's get to work!"

The three of us went into the living room, turning lights on along the way. Austin set the backpack on the floor and rummaged through it. He passed me an electromagnetic field (EMF) meter, and ultraviolet (UV) flashlight, and an electronic voice phenomenon (EVP) recorder. I looked at him with a big question mark on my face when he pulled out duplicates for himself.

"It's a big house," he stated. "We'll cover everything faster if we split up."

"Split up?" I hoped my voice cracking was detected by my ears only. I hated the idea of either one of us roaming this place alone.

Austin nodded. "I'll take the upstairs."

"I guess that leaves me down here," I said, trying to contain my nervousness.

"What about the cellar?" Jess asked.

The cellar. I felt the hair on my arms rise as images of Nathan in the rocking chair flashed through my mind. I'll admit the thought of going into that dark, eerie place again scared the living crap out of me. Who knew what was lurking down there now?

"We'll tag team it," Austin said, giving me a reassuring smile. I forced myself to smile back and nod in agreement.

"Is there anything I can help you guys with?" Jess asked.

"Stick with Ava. I'm sure she'll find something for you."

Disappointment and a hint of jealousy were clear on Jess's face as Austin turned his back to her and left the living room. I pressed my lips firmly together, holding in the laughter that threatened to come out. Jess turned to face me.

"Do you have any theories about what's going on here?"

I shrugged as I shoved the EVP and flashlight into my pockets. "We're not really sure yet."

She crossed her arms and tilted her head slightly. "Are you just saying that to avoid scaring me?"

"No." I shook my head. "We have our suspicions, but things are a little contradicting." Jess wrinkled her forehead in confusion. I let out a sigh and tried to explain myself a little better. "Some things you told us point toward poltergeist activity, but other things point toward. . .something else."

"Like what?"

"You don't want to know," I muttered, fumbling with the power switch on the EMF meter.

"You know, normally I'd beg you to tell me, but you're probably right," she admitted quietly, lowering her gaze to the floor.

"It'll be okay, though," I added quickly, seeing the deep concern on her face. "This isn't our first rodeo. Austin and I can get rid of anything." I ended with a smirk that showed way more confidence than I really felt.

"I hope so," Jess said as she looked at me with a smile that didn't quite reach her eyes.

Before beginning the investigation, I took a moment to look around the living room. Natural light flooded in through the large windows that faced the front and side of the house. There were two doorways: the one we'd entered through from the foyer and another that led into a corridor. A large flat-screen TV was mounted to a wall, with a cube storage unit underneath it. A large area rug with a gray-and-white abstract design was held down by a couch and two matching chairs that were aimed toward the TV.

"Can you show me where Brayden saw something the other day?" I asked Jess.

She nodded and walked toward the far end of the couch. Turning to face me, she said, "This is the general area." She pointed to a pile of toys a couple of feet from her. "We were sitting there."

Keeping the EMF meter pointed ahead, I walked toward her. There were no cold spots, no abnormal readings on the meter, no whispers in the wind, and certainly no monsters popping up and yelling, "Boo!" I continued walking around the living room in hopes that the EMF meter would pick up something, but to no avail.

"Have you noticed a pattern — like a certain time of day — that these paranormal events occur?" I asked Jess.

She shook her head. "No. They just happen randomly."

"Interesting."

I motioned for her to follow me as I headed through the other doorway. The corridor was fairly small, consisting only of a closet that held the washer and dryer. At the other end was the dining room. After walking in a giant circle around the table, we headed into the kitchen.

"Nothing seems out of the ordinary so far," I told her.

"I'm not surprised," she responded nonchalantly.

I narrowed my eyes at her. "Why?"

"Nothing ever happens when I'm home alone," she replied simply.

I cocked a single eyebrow. "Come again?"

She twisted a strand of hair around her finger while talking. "I don't know why, but when I'm home alone, everything's perfectly fine. It's only when my parents are around that things get. . .*weird*."

"When your parents are around or when your *dad* is around?" I emphasized for clarification.

"Um, well. . ." she shifted her weight and looked toward the ground.

"Damn it," I muttered angrily.

"That's not a good thing, is it?" she asked hesitantly.

Ignoring her question, I walked out of the middle doorway that led back into the foyer. "Come on. We need to find Austin."

On the way to the staircase, we passed the cellar door. Glancing at it for a moment, I wondered what was lying down there after all this time. In my mind, I imagined the old rocking chair, abandoned and eerily rocking on its own. Intense fear ran through me and I kicked it into high gear, bolting past the door and up the stairs.

I rounded the corner at the top just as Austin was exiting one of the bedrooms, causing us to collide into each other. He quickly grabbed my arms to keep me from falling backward.

"Damn, girl. Slow down," he said, chuckling.

"Sorry," I mumbled.

"Holy shit, Ava," Jess said from behind me, breathless from the quick trek upstairs. "You had me thinking the Devil was after you!"

"Did something happen?" Austin asked, his voice thick with concern as his eyes narrowed.

"No, um, I, uh, was just in a hurry to report my findings." Okay, so it was a terrible lie, but admitting the truth — that even looking at the cellar door scared the bejeezus out of me — meant we would have to confess *everything* to Jess right here, right now.

"Well, what did you find?" Austin urged.

"Um. . .nothing," I admitted lamely.

The corners of his mouth twitched upward as he fought to hold back his laughter. After clearing his throat, he said, "I didn't find anything here either."

"Actually, I just learned something that may explain that." I turned to Jess and gestured toward Austin. "Tell him what you told me."

She picked at her nails nervously. "Um, I've never witnessed any paranormal stuff when my dad is gone."

Austin's eyes widened. "Nothing at all?"

"No."

"So that must mean wha—"

His words were cut off by the sound of a door creaking downstairs. The three of us froze and exchanged confused glances. Then there was a noise that sounded like furniture being dragged across the floors and someone rummaging through cabinets. Had Melissa or Derek come home for some reason?

Then the noises stopped. A few seconds later, a door suddenly slammed shut, making the three of us jump in unison.

"W-what was that?" Jess whispered, a slight quaver to her voice.

"I don't know," Austin whispered back, furrowing his brow. "Let's go check it out."

The wooden stairs creaked and groaned under our weight as we went down them. If anyone had come home, they surely would have heard us and acknowledged our presence by now. But there were no signs of anyone else around.

Jess went to the front door and jiggled the knob. "This is still locked."

"Are there any other doors that lead outside?" Austin asked.

"There's one that leads out back in the study," Jess replied.

I pulled the investigation equipment out of my pockets. "You guys go check the other door. I'm going to put these away."

The instant I stepped into the living room, I knew something was off. It was like the feeling you get when you know your little sister has been in your room, snooping through your personal property to get the tea on the new guy you've been obsessing over, but everything looks the same so you can't prove it to your parents.

I looked around the room, trying to decide what was different. It wasn't until I went to put my equipment away that I noticed it.

Austin's backpack was gone.

"Well, hell." I sighed and ran a hand through my hair. Austin was *not* going to be happy about this.

"Ava!" I jumped at the sound of someone yelling my name from across the large house. Shoving the equipment back into my pockets, I quickly retreated from the living room.

"Ava, come here!" Austin called again with urgency.

I followed his voice to the kitchen. "I'm here, I'm here. Calm d—"

My eyes widened as my mouth gaped open unattractively. All the cabinet doors and drawers were wide-open, exposing all their neatly organized contents. Five chairs had been dragged in from the dining room and scattered a few feet apart between the island and the doorway that led from the foyer.

"Has this ever happened before?" I asked Jess.

She shook her head. "Things get moved around sometimes, but it's usually small items — nothing this extreme." She glanced back and forth between Austin and me. "What would have the ability to do this?"

"Any number of entities," Austin replied. He leaned against the island and crossed his arms over his chest. "This sort of behavior is most common with poltergeists, though."

"But those are harmless, right?" she asked.

"In most cases, yes."

Their conversation continued, but I wasn't paying attention. Instead I was focused on the chairs. Something about their placement was odd to me. . .or should I say, oddly *familiar*.

"Jess, do you have any string or masking tape?" I interrupted.

"There's some in the backpack," Austin replied instead.

"Yeah, about that," I began, drawing my words out slowly. "The backpack is kind of. . .gone."

"Gone!" he repeated loudly, looking at me in total disbelief. "Do you have any idea how many *thousands* of dollars' worth of equipment is in there?"

I lifted a single brow in his direction. "Considering I helped pay for some of it, yes." Then I looked at Jess, who hadn't moved an inch. "Tape, string, anything please."

"Oh, right!" She rummaged through the already open drawers. A few seconds later she produced a roll of green painter's tape. "Will this work?"

"Yes, that's perfect."

She tossed the roll to me, and I got to work placing strips of tape on the ground, marking the space between each chair. Austin was pacing back and forth, running a hand through his hair in frustration.

"I'm going to be here for a minute," I told him. "You two go search for the backpack. You called me in here before I had a chance to look. I may have just overlooked it."

"All right. Holler if you need me," Austin said before taking off toward the living room with Jess trailing behind.

I remained on the floor, crawling back and forth between the chairs. Thankfully, the roll of tape looked like it had hardly been used, so I was in no danger of running out. A slow, eerie creaking sound floated to me from the foyer. I whipped my head around but couldn't see past the doorway from my position.

"Austin?" I called out.

The creaking was replaced by the sound of footsteps. I finished laying the last strip of tape before standing up to investigate. I tiptoed toward the doorway; Austin and Jess were standing at the far end of the foyer, staring wide-eyed in my direction. My blood ran ice cold as I realized they weren't looking at me. They were looking at the cellar door, which now stood wide-open halfway between us.

"Did you guys open that?" I asked, surprised that my voice remained calm and even.

"We were in the living room," Austin replied. "I thought you did."

I shook my head. "It wasn't me."

"Then who was it?" Jess asked in a shaky voice.

Slowly, I looked behind me — half expecting a creepy, decaying corpse to be standing there like some horror movie cliché. Thankfully, no one was there, but what I *did* see had my jaw dropping to the floor as my heart beat rapidly in my chest. I'd been right to notice something strange about the placement of the chairs. From where I stood in the doorway of the kitchen, I gazed down upon a perfect inverted pentagram.

"What do you see?" Austin asked.

I drew in a shaky breath as I turned to face him once again. "Our suspicions are confirmed. The demon is definitely back."

CHAPTER EIGHT

"The *what* is back?" Jess screeched.

"Jess, it's okay," Austin told her as he rested a reassuring hand on her shoulder.

"Like hell it is!" she yelled, flinging her arms out to the side in exasperation. "Ava just said there is a D-E-M-O-N *demon* in my house!"

Ignoring her freakout, Austin headed in my direction. While passing the cellar door, he turned sideways and slid along the opposite wall as if he expected something to reach out and drag him into the pit of darkness. Once he got to the kitchen, he stood next to me and studied the pentagram.

"Well, that's new," he muttered while rubbing his chin.

"A pentagram?" Jess said as she stepped up to join us. "I thought those were symbols of good things."

"They are," Austin said. "But the *inverted* pentagram has been commonly seen as a symbol of evil. Whether it really means that or not doesn't matter right now, though. Whatever put these chairs here knew what it was doing, and knew that we would understand it's hidden message either way."

"But if this thing really is a. . .demon. . .then why would it announce itself so clearly?" she questioned.

"Who knows?" Austin sighed. "Let's check out the cellar. We'll come back to this later."

Hesitantly, Jess and I followed him into the foyer. As we stood before the open door, the musty smell of the cellar wafted up to me. I peered down into the darkness. Fear and anxiety made their way throughout my body; I shoved my hands into my pockets to hide their shaking.

Austin flicked on the light switch, casting bright light upon the old, rugged staircase. "Let's go."

Jess and I exchanged concerned looks, unsure this was a good idea. Austin was almost at the bottom by the time we worked up the courage to follow him.

The switch had also turned on a single light bulb that hung from the ceiling in the middle of the large room; barely illuminating the entire area. Empty wooden shelves lined most of the walls. Back in the day, they'd probably been filled with canning jars. I gasped and nearly tumbled backward into Jess when I spotted the rocking chair I'd found Nathan in. It now sat near a pile of boxes in the far corner of the room.

Austin flashed me a concerned look. I shrugged casually and mouthed out the word *clumsy* in an attempt to play off my fear as nothing more than my innate ability to trip over air.

"Is that your stuff?" I asked Jess, gesturing toward the corner.

"No. The previous owners left that here. We haven't had a chance to go through it yet."

As I stared at the boxes, my mind drifted off as I wondered what they contained. Perhaps someone had boxed up Carrie's knickknacks, which her grandmother had passed on to her. Surely someone would have snatched up Nathan's mint-condition *Star Wars* collection by now. I can't imagine little Riley roaming the afterlife without her blankie or Allie without her doll.

"Ava?" Austin's voice snapped me back to reality. "You okay?"

"I'm fine," I lied. I swallowed past the lump in my throat. "I was just wondering what could have been unimportant enough to leave behind like that."

Austin flashed me a sad smile before turning away. I felt Jess eye me suspiciously, probably wondering why such a scaredy cat would be involved in this line of work.

Maybe I should just tell her the truth. No! Not yet.

I mentally shook myself and returned my focus to the job at hand. Austin was walking toward a doorway to the right of the stairs that was covered by what looked like half of a worn-out bed sheet.

Turning to Jess, I said, "Start looking for anything out of the ordinary. If you see something, say something."

"Got it," she said, giving me a thumbs up.

I turned my EMF meter back on and began searching around the stairs. As I stepped to one side of the staircase, I spotted a small area behind it, but it was too dark to see much. I pulled out my cell phone and turned on the flashlight. Cobwebs stretched from the back of the stairs to the wall. I shined my light past them and sighed with relief when I spotted nothing worth walking through the webs for.

As I turned to head back toward the main area of the cellar, I caught a glimpse of something wedged beneath the bottom step. I lay on the ground to get a better look.

"Well, would you look at that?" I whispered to myself as I grabbed one of the straps of Austin's backpack and hauled it out.

It was covered in cobwebs, but at least it appeared to be full and in one piece. As I started to get up, something else caught my eye. I reached under the stairs where the backpack had been until the tips of my fingers brushed against the smooth, flat object. After a few attempts, I managed to get a grip and pulled it out.

I sat upright and looked at the photo in my hand. My hand flew up to cover my mouth as I stifled a sob. The Johnson family smiled back at me — carefree and happy, completely unaware they would soon meet their demise. I blinked fast, willing the tears to not overflow. For once, they listened.

Using the stairs as a support, I hauled myself back on my feet. I flung the backpack over one shoulder and — photo in hand — I headed back toward the main area of the cellar. Jess saw me from across the room and met me in the middle. Austin emerged from the covered doorway a few seconds later.

"Nothing in there," he announced. "Just an old boiler room."

"Look what I found," I said, swinging the backpack in front of me. Austin stormed over and snatched it from my grasp.

"Fucking demons!" he shouted angrily to the empty space behind him.

I swallowed my laughter and said, "I found it under the stairs." Then I handed him the photo. "Along with this."

Jess stepped closer to him, studying the photo. "Who are they?"

"The family who lived here before you — the Johnsons," I told her.

"You mean the ones you babysat for?"

I nodded. "Yeah, them."

"Those kids are so adorable!" she gushed. "Are they twins?"

"Yes, they were."

I pressed my lips together, realizing my mistake. Jess studied me closely. I averted my eyes from her, not wanting her to see the sadness within them. It felt like hours had passed before she broke the silence.

"They didn't really move, did they?" Jess asked softly.

Not trusting my own voice, I shook my head in response.

"If you knew they. . .you know. . .then why did you come back here looking for them?"

"We didn't," Austin replied for me.

Jess turned her attention to him. "But that's what you—"

"We lied," he admitted. "It was the only way we could get in here to investigate."

Confusion was written all over her face. "But you didn't know anything was going on until I told you. So why did you need to investigate?"

Austin sighed heavily. "Let's go upstairs where it's more comfortable. We'll explain everything."

In the living room, Austin and I sat next to each other on the couch while Jess plopped down on one of the matching chairs. Although I'd known this conversation would happen eventually, I was still unprepared for it. The only person — other than Austin — who knew of my past mistake was Samantha Foster. Sam had been kind and understanding when I'd told her. Would Jess be the same? After all, running out on the Johnsons didn't affect Sam in any way, but it had now put Jess's family in danger. I wouldn't blame her if she hated me and kicked me out before Austin and I finished the job.

"I hope you don't get scared or traumatized easily," Austin teased lightheartedly.

Jess smirked. "Try me."

Austin slid his hand into mine before giving a short nod, signaling the ball was in my court. I faced Jess and launched into the short, tragic story of the Johnson family. Of course, I cried like a baby during the retelling — who wouldn't? To my surprise, Jess remained silent and attentive the entire time. Once I finished spilling the tea *and* the beans everywhere, she finally spoke.

"Oh, my God," she breathed. Her eyes were filled with sadness, but I didn't detect any tears.

"I'll understand if you want us to go," I said.

"What?" she asked in disbelief. "Why would I want that?"

"Because your family is in danger thanks to me!" I cried in frustration.

"Ava, how could you think any of this is *your* fault?" She reached a hand out to grasp my arm. "You were inexperienced, alone, and scared. I'd never hold the past against you, and you shouldn't either."

Austin wrapped an arm around my shoulders. "She's right, you know."

I smiled through my tears at Jess. "Thank you." Then I turned to Austin. "I love you."

"I love you too, babe." He smiled back and gently kissed my forehead.

"So what brought you guys back here?" Jess asked.

"I've been having nightmares lately — flashbacks of that night," I explained. "I thought it might be an omen of things stirring up here again so we decided to check it out."

"Good thing we did," Austin added. "Turns out this house is death central."

Jess narrowed her eyes at him. "What the hell does that mean?"

"Well..." Austin began, stretching out the word. Then he launched into his own story, telling her everything he'd discovered about the previous owners and their tragic deaths — beginning with the original owner and his son's mysterious disappearance.

Once he was done, Jess let out a long breath. "Well, shit. That was unexpected."

"Tell me about it," I muttered, rolling my eyes. "I wonder how powerful this demon truly is."

"It doesn't matter," Austin said with a cocky grin. "We'll send it back to hell either way."

"I have full faith in you guys." Jess smiled. With a wink, she added, "Especially you, Ava."

"This is just like all the other exorcism cases," Austin told me. "We trap them, exorcise them, and then everyone lives happily ever after."

With a grin that exuded false confidence, I added, "Piece of cake."

CHAPTER
NINE

By now, there was no denying something spooky and demonic was going on in this house. But we still had a million unanswered questions. What could be keeping a demon in this house all these years? Was Derek possessed or just being an asshole? If the demon *was* inside him, then who had moved the dining room chairs, hidden the backpack, and opened the kitchen cabinets and drawers while he was at work?

Perhaps the demon comes and goes from him freely, I thought. It was conceivable but unlikely. Once a demon leaves its vessel, the human regains consciousness and can recall everything that happened before and during the possession. Surely if this were the case, Derek would have told Melissa something was wrong and they would have already fled the house.

"I guess it's a good thing you came up with that whole interview idea after all," I told Jess. "It looks like we'll have to stick around as long as possible to dig up more answers and complete our task."

"I know. I'm a genius," she said with a flip of her long, wavy hair.

"We still have a while before Melissa and Derek get home," Austin said, looking at the time on his phone. "Let's go get something to eat. My treat."

"Uh, maybe we should put the kitchen back together first," I suggested. "It's kind of a mess."

"Good idea," Jess agreed.

The three of us quickly cleaned up the kitchen, ensuring that it looked exactly as it did before a pain in the ass spook messed with it. Afterward, we all climbed into the Lexus and went to a nearby Wendy's for lunch. Spending time away from the house and the darkness surrounding it lifted our spirits. I was filled with renewed hope and confidence that all this would soon come to a complete end.

Before we knew it, it was time to head back to the house. When Melissa and Derek arrived home with Brayden, we were sitting in the living room, deep into our fake interview.

"It's good to see you two again." Melissa smiled warmly at Austin and me. "How's the interview coming along?"

"We're almost done," Jess told her.

"Do you mind if your brother plays in here while I cook dinner?"

"No problem."

Melissa sat Brayden on the floor near his toys. She passed him a few things to keep him occupied before leaving the room. While the tiny human played happily by himself, the three of us continued talking — keeping our voices low so Melissa and Derek wouldn't overhear us.

"Are you guys going to set up cameras?" Jess asked.

"No," Austin replied. "We've already witnessed the activity and know what it is. There's no time to further monitor things. We need to act, and fast. Who knows when the demon will decide it's had enough fun and games?"

"What's the plan then?" she asked.

"We need to confirm if the demon is in anyone right now or not," he said.

"How long will that take?"

Austin shrugged. "I don't know, but hopefully not too—"

"Hi!" Brayden said excitedly, bringing Austin's words to a grinding halt.

I whipped my head toward the doorway, expecting to see one of Jess's parents standing there, eavesdropping on our conversation. When I saw we were still alone, I let out a sigh of relief.

The top of Brayden's little blond head popped into my peripheral. I turned to look at him. He was now standing and facing the doorway that led to the laundry room corridor. Although I couldn't see his face, I imagined he was all smiles, judging by the bubbly laughter that emanated from him. I glanced at Austin and Jess, who were also focused on the interaction taking place between Brayden and the unknown.

"Is this what you were talking about before?" I asked Jess.

She nodded. "Yes."

I stood up and, with the EMF meter in hand, walked in the direction Brayden was looking. The meter lit up like a Christmas tree long before I stepped into the cold spot commonly produced by spirits. As the cool air brushed against my skin, I shivered. Taking a deep breath, I closed my eyes and let my other senses take over.

That's when I heard it. A woman's voice whispered in my mind, although it was too muddled to understand. The sweet sound of children laughing echoed Brayden's own laughter. An overwhelming sense of love and light floated around me. I didn't realize that I, too, was laughing and smiling until Austin spoke.

"Babe, what is it?"

My eyes opened and met his gaze. Pure joy filled me as I spoke. "This isn't a demon!"

"It's not?" he asked with a look of uncertainty.

I shook my head wildly. "I can hear them, feel them. They're *good*!"

"Then what was the inverted pentagram symbolizing?" he asked.

"And what's wrong with my dad?" Jess added.

Their questions caused the laughter in my head to quickly die out. All the joy that had surrounded me was instantly replaced with anger and a strong sense of protection. My expression involuntarily shifted to fit the new mood.

"Ava. . ." Austin began, but I held up a finger to silence him.

Closing my eyes again, I focused on the energies around me. A few seconds later, the woman's voice came to me again. It sounded like she was speaking through a tin can with background static, but I was able to make out some of the words.

Came back. . .warn. . .evil. . .get them out. . .too late.

My eyes flew open and immediately locked on Jess. "I think these little pranks — doors opening and objects moving — have been these good spirits trying to warn you about the demon since you moved in."

As if confirming my interpretation was correct, the spirits disappeared. The air around me returned to its normal temperature and the lights on the EMF meter went out.

"Spirits? As in more than one?" Jess asked in bewilderment.

I smiled and nodded. "Don't worry. These ones won't hurt you."

"This could be a good thing actually," Austin said, rubbing his chin thoughtfully.

"How?" Jess and I asked in unison.

"Well, I haven't dealt with a situation like this myself, but my old mentor once told me that positive energies weaken negative ones. So it only makes sense that having good spirits hanging around could weaken the demon."

I shrugged. "Makes sense to me."

Brayden had gone back to playing with his toys, and I returned to the couch. A couple of minutes later, Melissa poked her head into the room.

"Ava, Austin, would you guys like to stay for dinner?"

"Got anymore pie?" Austin grinned.

I nudged him with my elbow and threw him a *Be polite* look. Then I smiled at Melissa. "We'd love to stay. Thank you."

"It's my pleasure." She smiled in return. "And yes, Austin, there's still some pie left." She gave him a playful wink before turning to her daughter. "Jess, could you give me a hand in the kitchen?"

"Can't Dad help?" she complained in typical teenage fashion.

"He's tired and wants to relax for a bit."

Jess sighed dramatically and stood up. "Fine."

"We'll help too," I offered.

Jess carried her little brother as we all followed Melissa to the kitchen. Derek passed us in the foyer. Although his face appeared normal — friendly even — there was a darkness in his eyes. I crossed my arms over my chest, feeling an eerie discomfort as he brushed past me.

Before entering the kitchen, I glanced behind me. Derek was still standing in the foyer with his eyes focused directly on me. My entire body tensed up as my pulse quickened. The corners of his mouth slowly twitched upward into a mischievous grin. With a short, almost playful, chuckle that made my blood run cold, he tore his gaze from mine and disappeared into the living room.

"What's for dinner?" Austin asked eagerly, totally unaware of what just happened.

"Homemade lasagna and garlic bread," Melissa replied.

"Do you cook like this all the time?"

"Absolutely!" she said proudly. "There's nothing better than a home cooked meal."

Austin leaned against the counter and grinned at her. "Damn. Derek sure is one lucky guy."

"Hey!" I laughed as I smacked his arm. He winked at me and stuck his tongue out playfully.

"Jess, can you dig out the casserole dish?" Melissa asked while she grabbed a frying pan.

"Sure."

"Anything I can help with?" Austin asked.

"You can start dicing the onions and garlic I put over there." Melissa gestured toward the island. "Knives are over here by me and the cutting boards are under the island."

Austin followed instructions and began dicing. I was getting ready to offer a helping hand when Brayden came toddling up to me.

"Toys!" he shouted up at me.

"You want toys, buddy?" I asked as I knelt to his height. He nodded frantically; I couldn't help but giggle at his cuteness. "Okay. I'll go grab you some toys."

I stood up and made my way to the living room. As I got closer, I heard what sounded like a football game playing on the TV. I took a deep breath — preparing myself for another creepy and uncomfortable encounter with Derek — and stepped into the room. To my surprise, it was empty. I continued across the room to Brayden's toys.

As I rummaged through the pile, trying to find something to keep the little guy occupied for a while, my hand bumped a button on a play phone. It lit up in multicolored lights and played a little tune. Nearby was a small wooden box with holes in various shapes and sizes, filled with cutouts of the shapes.

I was debating which one would be the best option when suddenly I felt I was being watched. I whipped my head around, but still found myself completely alone. Feeling the strong urge to leave, I snatched up the phone and shape sorter.

As I began to walk away, I heard a sound like someone was tapping their fingernails on a solid surface. I paused mid-step to look around, but the noise had stopped. With my next step, the noise returned. I looked down at the toys in my hand and laughed. It was just the shapes moving inside the box!

"You're losing it, Ava," I said, chuckling to myself.

I was almost to the doorway when the TV turned to static, stopping me in my tracks. But the tapping continued. That's when I realized the sound wasn't coming from the box in my hand — it was coming from *above* me.

My heart pounded rapidly as goosebumps covered my body. Slowly, hesitantly, I tilted my head upward. Derek was crouched upside down on the ceiling, looking every bit like Spider-Man: Demon Edition. His head was tilted at an unnatural angle while his dark eyes bored into mine, unblinking. Black, smoky tendrils snaked out of his orifices, reminding me of the smoke that surrounded the house in my nightmares.

I opened my mouth to scream, but no sound came out. Stumbling over my own feet, I sprinted from the room.

Jess was the first one to catch sight of me as I entered the kitchen. I must have looked as freaked out as I felt because her mouth flopped open and she nearly dropped the can of tomato sauce in her hands. She immediately began distracting her mom to keep her from suspecting anything. Austin ran over to me, taking the toys from my clammy, trembling hands. He passed them to Brayden before ushering me into the dining room.

"What's wrong?" His voice was thick with concern.

"D-Derek is definitely p-possessed," I said, still panting from the adrenaline pumping throughout my body.

"What happened? What did you see?"

I inhaled deeply and told him everything in one long breath. As I spoke, his expression changed from concerned to intrigued then slightly amused.

"Huh," he mused as he rubbed the back of his neck. "I've seen possessed people do a lot of freaky things, but that's a new one." He gave me his adorable cocky grin. "Sounds pretty badass, though."

I lifted one shoulder and managed to crack a smile. "Yeah, it kind of was."

"Stay here," he said. "I'll see if he's still there."

Austin disappeared down the corridor that led into the living room. A few seconds later, he came back looking more than a little confused.

"Was he in there?" I asked.

"Yeah, watching a football game."

"Great," I grumbled. "Now I sound insane."

Austin chuckled and wrapped an arm around me. "Hey, I believe you. At least now we have our proof and we know what to do next."

"We need to trap him and exorcise the shit out of him," I said with determination.

His eyes sparkled as he smiled proudly. "That's my girl. Together we'll send that motherfucker back where it belongs."

"Hell yeah!"

I was beyond ready to put this nightmare to an end. Little did I know, the real nightmare was just about to begin. . .

CHAPTER TEN

Melissa's lasagna was the best I'd ever tasted! I couldn't understand why Derek accused her of being a bad cook before. Of course, Austin enjoyed the apple pie more than anything. I was relieved Derek remained normal long enough to enjoy the delicious meal with us.

Jess kept a cautious eye on him the entire time — no doubt worried that he'd turn into freaky spider-demon again at any given moment. Okay, maybe I should have waited until *after* we ate to tell her about her father being the demon's latest cozy vessel, but I'm not exactly the sharpest tool in the shed at times. Thankfully, Melissa didn't suspect anything out of the ordinary.

After we all finished eating, I helped Melissa clean up while Austin and Jess spent time with Brayden in the living room. The plan was for me to have one-on-one time with her in hopes of finding a way to bring up the whole you-and-your-family-need-to-leave-because-your-husband-is-possessed topic. No matter how I brought it up I was sure to sound completely insane, but I needed to do it to allow Austin and me more time in the house to perform an exorcism. Derek surely knew we were onto him by now. I feared the worst would happen if Austin and I stepped outside of this house again before the deed was done.

"Thank you for dinner," I told Melissa as I carried a stack of dirty dishes from the dining room into the kitchen. "I apologize for intruding. . .*again*."

"It's really no bother." She smiled that warm, motherly smile at me. "Jess seems to enjoy having you guys here. She hasn't had much luck making friends since we moved."

"Being the new kid isn't easy," I said. "But Broken Arrow isn't too far from here. I'd be happy to come hang out with her anytime."

"I'm sure she'd love that!"

"If Austin tags along, I may have to start paying you for pies, though," I joked.

Melissa laughed as she rolled up her sleeves and put dishes into the warm, soapy water. Bruises lining one of her forearms caught my eye. I maneuvered myself to get a closer look without being too suspicious. My eyes widened as I recognized the shapes and pattern of the bruises. They were fingerprints, created by someone grabbing her arm a little too hard.

I gestured toward her arm. "What happened there?"

"Oh, um, I don't really know," she replied awkwardly. "My iron has been a little low lately I guess."

"They look sort of like fingerprints, don't you think?" I tried to make my tone sound casual.

"Well, you know how toddlers are — always grabbing things like it's their lifeline." She laughed nervously, keeping her eyes on the water instead of looking at me. Lying certainly wasn't her strong point. Those marks were way too big to have been caused by Brayden.

I debated telling her about Jess witnessing Derek hit her, but I decided to steer the conversation in another direction. Being chased out of the house and getting Jess in trouble were two things I wanted to avoid at all costs.

"So, uh, have you noticed anything strange happening since you moved in?" I asked.

Melissa looked at me questioningly. "Like what?"

"Creaking in the attic, doors opening on their own — you know, spooky stuff."

She thought for a moment. "Yeah, I guess I've noticed some of that." Then she shrugged. "But it's an old house. It's bound to have drafts and make noises here and there."

While her response was logical, I knew the happenings in this particular house were caused by something paranormal. How could I get a non-believer to see that, though? As if on cue, I saw a movement out of the corner of my eye. I turned my head to see the refrigerator door slowly opening on its own. When I looked at Melissa, she was staring past me toward the fridge with her mouth gaped open.

"Let me guess — it's just a draft?"

Melissa's face flushed with embarrassment as she walked past me to shut the door. "Okay, so maybe not *everything* that happens has a logical explanation."

"Actually, it does," I told her.

"Are you suggesting a ghost did that?"

I nodded. "But you don't believe in them, do you?"

"I didn't used to," she replied so quietly I struggled to hear her.

"What changed your mind?"

"This house," she admitted. "I see and hear things that aren't there. Stuff like that happens"—she gestured toward the refrigerator—"and I can't explain it any other way."

"Has Derek noticed anything?" I asked.

Melissa's eyes turned sad as she shrugged. "He hasn't been the easiest person to talk to since we moved. In Phoenix, I could confide in him about everything." She scoffed. "But with the way he's been acting lately, he'd probably try to put me in a mental institution if I even dared suggest this place was haunted."

"So he doesn't believe in ghosts either?"

She shook her head. "He's even more close-minded about it than I am. It would be nearly impossible to make him believe in it."

Not as impossible as you think. I had to press my lips together to keep from saying my thoughts out loud. Once Austin and I got that demon out of him, he'd have no choice but to believe in the paranormal — the good *and* the bad.

"Judging by this conversation, I'm assuming you believe in this stuff, though," Melissa said.

"Yes, I do." I took a deep breath and the truth spilled out. "Austin and I aren't who you think we are." Melissa squinted her eyes suspiciously. "I don't work in retail and Austin isn't a personal trainer." *Even though he definitely has the body of one.* "We're paranormal investigators."

A slow, knowing smile spread across her face. "That's how Jess recognized you guys. She's always watching those ghost hunting shows."

"Yeah." I chuckled lightly, relieved that she wasn't mad. "I'm sorry we didn't tell you the truth sooner, but we weren't sure how you'd take it."

"I appreciate the honesty." Her eyes widened as if she just put the pieces together. "That's why you're here, isn't it? To hunt down the ghost in this house?"

I nodded slowly. "Yes, it is."

"The family you babysat for—"

"I didn't really babysit for them," I admitted. "But I *did* know the previous owners. I tried to help them three years ago."

"Tried?" she repeated, confused. "Are you saying you can't get rid of this thing?"

"Oh, no. I'm not saying that at all," I assured her quickly.

"So you can do it?"

I met her steady gaze. "I *can* and I *will*. I give you my word."

There was no backing out now; I wouldn't run away this time. I'd stand my ground and fight for my life and theirs — no matter the cost.

CHAPTER ELEVEN

Once I finished helping Melissa in the kitchen, it was time to fill Austin and Jess in on our conversation. But first, I needed a bathroom break. So instead of turning left in the foyer to go into the living room, I took a right.

The short detour gave me time to think of a plan to tell Melissa that her husband was possessed — a little detail I failed to mention during our conversation. I could only hope she'd believe me. With Austin and Jess there to back me up, there was no way she could *not* believe us. Either way, I also needed a plan to get Melissa, Jess, and Brayden out of the house. Although it wouldn't be easy, it was crucial to ensure their safety while Austin and I performed the exorcism on Derek. Not only could the demon kill all of us in the blink of an eye, but they are also tricky and would gladly play a game of musical vessels if given the chance. So the fewer humans around the better.

By the time I reached the bathroom, I still didn't have a plan. I sighed heavily as I stepped inside and turned to close the door. A foot suddenly wedged itself into the doorway, preventing me from fully closing the door.

"What the. . .?" I began as I took a step back, away from the door.

It swung open with such force that the doorknob left a small dent in the old wall. Then Derek stepped into the bathroom with me. He closed the door and slid the lock into place. When he turned to face me, his eyes were solid black and his mouth was pulled back into a snarl.

"What do you want?" I demanded.

His humorless laughter filled the small, enclosed space and sent shivers down my spine. "Don't play games with me, Princess. You know *exactly* what I want."

"You want me to leave you alone so you can kill this family just like you've killed all the others before them."

Derek cocked his head slightly, rubbing his chin. "Why do you have to make it sound so. . .*terrible*?"

"Because it *is* terrible, you piece of shit!" I screamed at him.

In a split second, he was mere inches from my face, gripping my chin in his cold hand. His foul breath blasted me in the face as he spoke, causing my stomach to churn. "Tsk-tsk. Didn't your mommy ever teach you manners?"

"Fuck you," I said through gritted teeth.

"Apparently she didn't," he grumbled in displeasure. His hand tightened on my chin, causing me to flinch slightly. "Look here, *Princess*. You tried to stop me before and failed miserably. I won't let you succeed this time either."

I rolled my eyes and scoffed. "You and what army?"

Derek released my chin and paced in front of the door, still blocking my only exit. "I'll admit, you weren't a threat to me before, but I sense a change in you," he mused out loud. "You're much more arrogant than I remember. Stronger too." He gestured toward the door. "And that little *boy toy* of yours is nearly as strong as you."

"He's not my boy toy," I snarled.

"Regardless," he said, raising his voice to show authority, "you two being here poses a threat to me and my plans."

"Good," I said smugly.

Derek stopped pacing and faced me. "Despite your lack of manners and respect toward me, I've decided to be nice and give you a chance to leave here. . .*alive*. You have two options." He held up one finger. "One, you and your little friend can leave this house and never look back. Or two —" he held up a second finger — "you both can stay here and perish with the rest of the family." He raised one brow in my direction. "Which will it be?"

"I choose to send you back to hell where you belong!"

"That's not an option," he snapped.

I raised my chin slightly and straightened my spine, asserting dominance. "I won't choose anything else."

"Very well then," he said solemnly.

His eyes closed as he stretched his arms out to the side, palms upward. I saw his lips move but couldn't hear the words he spoke. Within a few seconds, black tendrils formed in his palms. They swirled around in his hands, looking like little whirlpools of darkness.

"What's happening?" I asked, my voice shaking as fear overtook me.

"You didn't choose, so I'm deciding for you," Derek said simply, opening his eyes to look at me. He tilted his palms downward in my direction. Hundreds of demonic tendrils shot out from his hands toward the floor between us.

"No! You can't do this!" I could barely hear my own words over the pounding in my chest.

The tendrils came together and formed a shadowy figure. It quickly grew to my height and took on the shape of a human.

Derek's mouth twitched up into an evil grin. "I'm not usually so dramatic about this, but it's so much fun."

"Austin!" I screamed at the top of my lungs.

"Scream all you want. Nobody can hear you."

Suddenly the shadow figure lurched forward and wrapped its arms around me. I struggled to free myself, but it was too powerful for me to fight off. Tendrils worked their way into my nostrils and ears, leaving behind a burning sensation that had me writhing in agony. Despite Derek's words, I screamed for Austin again, but the sound was quickly cut off by a tendril shooting into my mouth. I coughed and gagged as it made its way down my throat. Tears streamed down my face as I realized this was the end.

I caught one last glance at Derek. With a victorious look, he said, "See you on the flip side, Princess."

Then my world turned to black.

PART TWO
Austin

CHAPTER TWELVE

I was having a blast helping Brayden create a tower out of his giant plastic building blocks. Spending time with the little guy made me long for the day I could become a dad. I only wish that I could be half as good of a dad as mine is. With Ava by my side, I know I will be. She brings out the best in me — always has and always will. I can't imagine getting married, having kids, and growing old with anyone else.

"Alright, Bray." Melissa crouched beside her son. "Bath time and then bed."

"'Kay!" With a giggle, Brayden threw himself into his mother's arms. As they left the room, he looked at me over Melissa's shoulder and waved. "Bye, Aus-in."

With a smile, I waved back. "Bye!"

I began tearing down the tower so Brayden could get a fresh start the next time he played with the blocks. Jess was engrossed in some dramatic reality show playing on

TV and hardly paying attention to my existence for once. Not that I minded. Sheesh, that girl was starting to get on my nerves with her obvious crush on me.

Suddenly I had the creepy-crawly feeling of something sinister lurking nearby. I glanced over my shoulder to see Ava standing in the doorway, looking mildly uncomfortable as her eyes darted around the room.

"Hey, babe," I said as I stood up. "What's wrong?"

"Huh? Nothing. Why?" She spoke quickly, still avoiding eye contact.

I shrugged. "You just look a little. . .*off.*"

"I'm fine," she snapped.

"Okay," I dragged the word out. "So how did the conversation with Melissa go?"

"That's none of your business."

I narrowed my eyes, studying her closely. Her straight, dark-blonde hair was a little disheveled and she looked completely worn out. This case was definitely taking a lot out of her. As much as I hated the idea of leaving here before exorcising Derek, Ava was obviously in need of some rest.

"Maybe we should go back to the hotel for the night and finish this case tomorrow," I suggested, lightly touching her arm.

"I'm not leaving," she stated firmly, moving away from my touch.

"Well, as long as you think you're alert enough to—"

She cut me off coldly. "*You're* more than welcome to leave, though."

"Are you kidding? I'm not leaving you here alone."

Her hazel eyes finally met mine. They weren't full of her usual love and happiness; instead, there was a strangely familiar darkness about them. She crossed her arms stubbornly, standing her ground.

"You can and you will," she said. When I opened my mouth to argue she put a hand up, signaling me to stop. "You're simply not needed here anymore, Austin."

"What?" I asked in disbelief. *What the hell is she talking about?* "Babe, what's going on with you?"

"Don't call me babe," she hissed. My stomach clenched at her words.

"What the fuck, Ava!" Jess's voice was brimming with anger as she stepped up beside me.

"What are you upset about?" Ava asked Jess, looking her up and down with disgust. "You haven't been able to keep your eyes off him since we got here. Hell, you've followed him around like a lost puppy half the time. You, of all people, should be *thrilled* about this."

Jess's face turned bright red with embarrassment. Her bottom lip began to tremble as tears welled up in her eyes. I wasn't sure if it was from humiliation or anger — or maybe both.

I closed the distance between Ava and me, grabbing her arms tightly and forcing her to look at me. "Look, I get that you're tired and angry at this entire situation, but you're taking it out on the wrong people! Save this anger and attitude for the demon!"

"The demon?" Ava threw her head back and laughed. "Oh, please. I have plenty of built-up resentment to throw at *the demon*." She put air quotes around the word.

Rolling her eyes, she said, "Seriously, Austin. How stupid do you have to be to realize I. Don't. *Want*. You. Here."

It felt like she had punched a hole in my chest. A lump formed in my throat, making it difficult to speak. "Y-you don't w-want. . ."

"No," she replied irritably, running a hand through her hair. Then she waved dismissively in my direction and added in a voice cold as ice, "Just go home. I never want to see you again."

Then Ava — the love of my life — turned around and walked out of my life, causing my heart to shatter into a million pieces. The weight of the world suddenly felt much too heavy, causing me to drop to my knees. I buried my face in my hands as the dam inside me broke. Tears poured down my cheeks, soaking my T-shirt and dripping to the floor. I continued to let it all out until I was left gasping for air.

"Okay, *Alice*, it's time to stop crying now," Jess said sarcastically.

I glared at her angrily. How could she be making jokes at a time like this? Reading my thoughts through my expression, she sighed heavily and knelt in front of me.

"I'm sorry," she said sincerely, resting a comforting hand on my shoulder. "But you really do need to stop crying and breathe." She stood up. "I'm going to find Ava and talk to her."

"No!" I choked out as I rose to my feet and grabbed her arm to prevent her from leaving. "Just let her be."

"You can't be serious!"

I used my shirt to wipe my tear-soaked face. "Look, I want nothing more than to find her and beg her to forgive me for whatever the hell I did wrong. But I have another job to do right now."

"Oh, my god!" Jess groaned in frustration, flinging her arms out to the side. "She's all in love with you, gets freaked out by Dad, spends one-on-one time with Mom, and then suddenly doesn't want a damn thing to do with you? That's not *strange* to you?"

All I could manage was to stare blankly at her while my brain processed her words. Of course I thought it was strange, but what could be the reason other than she simply didn't want me in her life anymore?

Maybe she's possessed.

No. That couldn't be it. There's only one demon in the house. If Ava were possessed, that would mean Derek wasn't, which also means he would remember everything. He would no doubt have been running around the house in full-blown panic mode trying to usher everyone out by now if that were the case.

Jess shook her head in disgust. "You're such an idiot. I'm going to figure this shit out whether you like it or not."

Before I had a chance to argue against it, she turned and walked out of the room. Left alone to deal with this unbearable pain, I walked over to the couch and sat down heavily. What the hell was going on? Why would Ava just up and walk out on me like that? And during a case of all times!

I should go find her. . .

No! She'd made it clear that she didn't want me anymore. If I went after her now, it would only make things worse. This family didn't need more negativity surrounding them.

But how could I let the only woman I've ever loved go so easily?

So many questions flooded my mind, yet no real answers came. Feeling overwhelmed, I rested my face in my hands as I tried to stifle the sobs that overcame me once again. I don't know how long I sat there like that. It felt like I was lost in my own bubble of depression and heartache for an eternity.

"Austin."

My head snapped up and I saw Jess standing in front of me. I hadn't even heard her come into the room. She looked concerned and confused.

"What's wrong now?" I asked, dreading her response.

"Ava is gone."

"What do you mean *gone*?" I asked firmly.

"I mean she's missing. I've searched everywhere for her!"

"Did you try calling her?"

She nodded. "It keeps going straight to voicemail."

"Damn it." I stood up and walked over to the large bay window that overlooked the front yard. My Lexus was still there. I turned back to Jess. "She couldn't have gone far unless she hitched a ride."

Jess looked at me, her brown eyes full of sadness and worry. "Are you going to leave us too?"

The idea was intriguing. After all, I was weak and vulnerable right now — even more so knowing Ava was missing. What good would I be against a powerful demon in this state? But if I left, I'd surely be playing into the demon's little game, and the results would be tragic. Besides, I came here to help Ava put an end to this crap and ease her troubled mind from her past. She could walk out on me all she wanted, but I'd never stop loving her and helping her any way I could.

My jaw clenched and unclenched. "No. I came here to do a job and I'm not leaving until it's done. No matter what."

CHAPTER THIRTEEN

"Sorry it took me a bit to get here. I just finished putting Brayden to bed," Melissa said as she entered the living room. She took a good look at me and her voice filled with motherly concern. "What's going on?"

I'd asked Jess to bring her in here. Since Ava wouldn't tell me about their conversation, it was up to me to find out for myself. Jess sat in her usual chair while Melissa sat beside me on the couch.

"Are you okay? Jess told me Ava is missing."

"She broke up with me," I said quietly. More tears threatened to escape, but I forced them back.

"Oh, Austin," Melissa breathed as she wrapped a comforting arm around my shoulders. "I'm so sorry."

"I'll be fine," I lied. Pushing my heartbreak aside temporarily, I took a deep breath and continued. "Ava was supposed to talk to you about—"

"About this house being haunted," Melissa finished for me. "She did."

"Oh, well, good," I said, a little surprised at how calm Melissa sounded about it. "Did she tell you who we really are?"

"Yes," she admitted with a slight smile. "You're paranormal investigators."

"And why they're really here?" Jess added questioningly.

Melissa nodded. "Ava was unable to get rid of the ghost before the last family moved, so you guys are back to finish the job."

"Um. . .that's not exactly. . ." Jess started hesitantly.

I opened and closed my mouth a few times, unsure how to tell her the truth. "Uh, Melissa," I began, shifting awkwardly in my seat. "There's something you should know. . ."

"What is it?" she asked, knitting her brow.

"The family who lived here before you didn't move away. They were killed by a demon who still resides here after Ava backed out of the case."

Melissa burst into hysterical laughter. "You're telling me a demon killed an entire family?" I nodded, making her laugh even more. "Oh, come on you guys. Ghosts are one thing. But a *demon*?"

"They're real and there's one in this house right now," I told her firmly.

Maybe it was the tone of my voice or perhaps the dead-serious look on my face, but Melissa's laughter quickly died out.

"Demons are evil, though," she pointed out. "If one is in this house, why hasn't anything bad happened?"

"Actually, something bad *has* happened," I informed her. "Ava was able to determine there are good spirits here too. It seems they have been trying to warn you — to scare you off — so the demon can't hurt you. Unfortunately, their warnings went unheard and now your husband is possessed by the demon."

"What!" she screeched, shaking her head wildly. "No! that's impossible! Derek could never—"

"I know about Dad hitting you," Jess cut in. "I saw it happen, Mom! You know as well as I do he hasn't been himself lately. He's changed, and not in a good way."

"No! He's just stressed out from this new job," Melissa argued.

"Ava saw him on the ceiling earlier," I blurted then pressed my lips together. I hadn't meant to tell her that. Not yet at least.

She looked at me with wide eyes. "What did you say?"

"Look, I know it sounds absolutely insane, but trust me. It happened. Derek was on the ceiling."

Melissa squeezed her eyes shut and bowed her head. It wasn't until I noticed tear stains forming on her navy-blue sweatpants that I realized she was crying.

"Melissa?" I said gently.

"Mom?" Concern was obvious in Jess's voice.

"I-Ithoughtitwasjustabaddream,"Melissawhispered.

"What are you talking about?" Jess asked curiously, moving to sit on the other side of her mom.

Melissa lifted her head and wiped the tears from her eyes. "It was one night last week. I woke up and found myself alone in bed. I figured Derek had either gone to the bathroom or gotten up earlier than usual. So I decided to go look for him."

She paused to take in a shaky breath. "I couldn't find him anywhere, so I went back to bed. After a bit, I heard someone come into the room. I opened my eyes and Derek was standing at the foot of the bed, just *staring* at me." Her forehead wrinkled. "Then out of nowhere he started *floating* up to the ceiling!"

Her hands trembled as tears rolled down her face. "I watched him crawl along the ceiling like a gigantic spider. He left the room and a few seconds later I heard a door slam shut downstairs."

I glanced at Jess, who was staring at her mom with one hand covering her mouth. Clearly, this was news to both of us. I turned back to Melissa. "What did you do next?"

"I hid under the blankets like a child," she admitted. "I kept convincing myself I was having a bad dream. When I woke up again, Derek was sleeping beside me as if nothing had happened."

"You said a door slammed downstairs," I recalled. "Do you know which one?"

Melissa shook her head. "It sounded like the cellar door, but there wasn't any reason for him to go down there."

"That would be an odd place to go," I agreed, rubbing my chin thoughtfully.

"So you believe us about the demon now?" Jess asked her mom.

"I have no choice." Melissa sighed in defeat, then she looked at me. "How do we help my husband?"

"I need you and Jess to get Brayden and leave the house."

"But—"

I raised my hand, cutting her off. "I have to exorcise the demon. It's already going to be difficult and risky enough on my own — I can't put you guys in more danger too."

"I made a vow to my husband — for better or worse, till death do us part," Melissa said firmly. "I'm not leaving him behind when he needs me the most."

"Look—" I started, but Jess cut in.

"I'm not leaving either."

I let out a long, frustrated breath. "You guys are in *serious* danger here!"

"You said it yourself: it won't be easy on your own," Jess pointed out. "If you let us stay, you won't be alone."

"Do either of you know anything about exorcising a demon?" I asked, exasperated at this point.

"Well, no," Jess admitted with a shrug. "But you can tell us what to do."

"Jess is right," Melissa said.

I let out a defeated sigh. "Fine. But if things get too out of hand, promise me you'll run like hell."

Jess gave me a tight nod. "We promise."

"Now what do you need us to do?" Melissa asked.

I took a few deep breaths, forcing my concerns about Ava out of my mind. Once I had total focus on the job at hand, I reflected back on everything I had learned so far about the house and the demon within it. Nothing explained what brought it here and why it has remained here all these years, feasting on innocent human souls. Derek needed to be trapped and exorcised, but I couldn't shake the feeling it would do no good.

"I feel like we're missing something," I said.

"Like what?" Jess asked.

"I'm not sure." I sighed and ran a hand through my hair. "This demon has been around for almost a century now. I've never known one to hang around the same place that long. Something has to be holding it here."

"That's bad, right?" Melissa asked.

"Very," I replied. "It means it could be even more difficult to get rid of it — if not impossible."

Melissa tilted her head slightly. "So how do we find out what's holding it here?"

"We look for strange things, like unusual symbols. Once we find something, we destroy it. Doing so should at least weaken the demon, if not completely eliminate it."

"Okay, well, where should we start?"

I immediately knew the answer. "The cellar."

"But we al—" Jess stopped abruptly and glanced at her mom, who was still unaware that she had skipped school so Ava and I could investigate the house. Jess cleared her throat. "Never mind. So why the cellar?"

"That's where Ava found Nathan Johnson hanging out when he was possessed. Plus, it's most likely where Derek went that one night," I explained.

And it's where Ava found my backpack, I added to myself.

"What are we waiting for?" Melissa asked, standing up. "Let's go check out the cellar."

As the three of us headed to the cellar, I kept glancing around in hopes of catching sight of Ava somewhere. No such luck. Wherever she was, I prayed she was safe.

Once we were inside the cool, dimly lit cellar, I told Melissa to search around the perimeter of the room and inside the boiler room. From our previous search, I already knew nothing was there, but it kept her occupied so I could talk to Jess without accidentally getting the kid in trouble.

"We already looked down here," Jess whispered to me once her mom was out of earshot.

"I know, but I feel like we missed something," I whispered back. "Of all places in this house to hide something, someone hid my backpack *down here*. It seems like an obvious sign to me."

"Good point. But we checked everywhere and found nothing."

"Actually, we didn't check everywhere."

Jess's face was a huge question mark. "Huh?"

"We didn't look through there." I gestured toward the pile of boxes in the corner of the room. "Isn't it a little strange that everything in this place was cleared out except those?"

"Well, yeah, kind of."

"So maybe something is hidden among it all that we aren't meant to see."

"But you said this demon has been around for almost a century. This crap has only been here since the last family died," Jess said.

I rubbed the back of my neck and sighed. "You have a point, but I still think it's worth checking out."

"All right," she agreed reluctantly. "It's a lot of stuff, though. It could take a while."

"Melissa," I called across the room. She turned to look at me. "Will you help us go through this junk?"

"Sure," she replied as she came to join us. "Are we actually going *through* the boxes or just moving them?"

"Both," I told her. "We need to be thorough."

We each grabbed a box and sifted through them. As we finished each one, we placed it off to the side. I found dishes, knickknacks, photo albums, and even a box full of scary-ass antique dolls that was sure to give me nightmares of my own, but no strange symbols or anything out of the ordinary.

It felt like the number of boxes multiplied every time I grabbed another from the pile. Several minutes later, the back wall came into view. That is when I noticed it. A strip of what appeared to be wood stuck out above the back row of boxes.

"Hey, I see something!" I announced. "Jess, come help me move these boxes."

She obeyed without question. We only needed to move a handful of boxes to expose the small, wooden door situated about waist-high on the wall. An old, rusty padlock held it shut.

"Did you guys know there was a dumbwaiter in the house?" I asked curiously as I didn't recall seeing one upstairs.

"No," Melissa replied as she came over to us.

"A dumb what?" Jess asked.

"A dumbwaiter," I repeated. "It's a system commonly used way back when in bigger homes to deliver stuff from floor to floor." I studied the ceiling, trying to determine where the dumbwaiter would lead to, but my sense of direction isn't the best. "There's nothing like this at all upstairs?"

"Not that I've ever seen," Melissa said.

I bet they removed most of it, or at least covered the doors, when they remodeled the house. It made sense to leave this portion of it. After all, it was built into the brick foundation. It would have been a hassle to take it out. But why lock it?

"I need something to break this lock," I said.

"Why not pick it?" Jess asked.

"I didn't bring my kit down here."

"Here," Melissa said, reaching into her hair and pulling out a bobby pin. "Try this."

I took the pin from her and attempted to pick the lock, but there was too much rust in the way. I kicked the lock a couple of times, causing some of the rust to rain down on the concrete floor below. Once the keyhole was more visible, I tried to pick it again. It took longer than usual, but I eventually got it open.

The lock was slightly rusted to the latch, so I had to use a little force to remove it. As soon as it was off, I swung the door open. My jaw dropped in surprise.

"Well, that definitely looks unusual to me," Jess said, stepping up beside me to study the interior.

Someone had painted (at least I *hoped* it was paint) a red circle with an inverted pentagram in the center on the floor of the dumbwaiter. Strange symbols I did not recognize were randomly drawn around the pentagram. The outer edge of the circle was lined with what appeared to be Latin words. Unfortunately, the only Latin I knew was the exorcism prayer. *Damn it, Ava. I could really use you right now.*

"What is it?" Melissa asked from the other side of me.

"It looks like a sigil, but I'm not sure what it me—"

"You're not supposed to be down here!" a voice boomed from behind us.

I spun around to find Ava standing at the bottom of the stairs. Her body was rigid and her face was set in anger. My heart ached at the sight. *Did she really hate me that much?*

"Well, well, well. Look who finally showed up to the party," Jess announced sarcastically.

"Shut up, bitch," Ava snapped at her.

"Don't you *dare* talk to my daughter like that!" Melissa yelled as she quickly approached Ava — ready to smack the shit out of her no doubt.

I could barely make out the evil sneer that crossed Ava's face from where I stood. Once Melissa was within her reach, Ava reached out with one hand, grabbed the front of her shirt, and easily lifted her into the air.

"What are *you* going to do about it?" she snarled, then tossed Melissa to the floor like a ragdoll. "You're just a weak, pathetic human."

Jess ran over to her mom. Glaring at Ava, she yelled, "What the fuck is wrong with you?"

Ignoring her, Ava shifted her eyes to me. "Why are *you* still here? I told you to go home."

"Yeah, well, that's too damn bad," I sneered as I took a few steps toward her. "Because unlike you, I don't leave people to die at the hands of a demon."

I immediately regretted my words when I saw a flash of pain in Ava's eyes. Just because she hurt me didn't give me the right to be a dick to her. I opened my mouth to apologize, but stopped when I saw her expression darken even more. The corners of her mouth tilted upward into a devilish grin as her eyes turned to solid black.

"You're going to regret not listening to me," she snarled, her voice deepening.

My eyes widened in realization as pure rage took over. "Son of a bitch! You possessed my girlfriend!"

CHAPTER FOURTEEN

I charged forward, ready to take on the demon in hand-to-hand battle — as if I stood a chance. Sarcastic laughter burst from Ava's mouth; the sound of it made me sick. I wanted nothing more than to make it stop. Without thinking, I punched her in the face as hard as I could.

"Austin, stop!" Jess yelled, yanking me backward by my shirt.

"I'm going to kick your ass, you demonic piece of shit!" I screamed.

"You can't do that," Jess said, holding my arm tightly as if she was really strong enough to hold me back. "Not while it's inside Ava at least."

I glared at her, pissed that she was getting in the way. "What the hell are you talking about?"

"You can't hurt me without hurting my vessel," Ava smirked proudly.

"As much as I hate to admit it, Black Eyes here is right," Jess said, gesturing toward Ava.

If I'd been thinking rationally, I would have known that without being told. The demon was only the entity inside. Anything I did to it physically would only damage the human shell concealing it. I glared angrily into the eyes of the demon possessing my girlfriend.

"Why her?" I demanded to know. "Was Derek no longer satisfactory for you?"

"Actually, I quite enjoy this vessel," another voice said from the top of the stairs. I looked up to see Derek coming down to join us.

My body became tense as my jaw dropped to the floor. Jess spoke the words I was thinking. "There are *two* demons in here?"

"Why must humans refer to us with such a derogatory term? I prefer *guardians of hell*." Derek dismissively waved a hand and looked at me. "But to answer your question, dear Austin, your precious little Ava was chosen because she was too much of a threat. She's much stronger this time."

"Why didn't you just let us go then?" I spoke through gritted teeth.

His head jerked back in surprise. "I gave her the option to leave here with you and never look back, but" — he shrugged and turned to Ava, reaching a hand out to brush the blonde hair from her face — "she chose to be the vessel for my lover, Victoria, instead." He wrapped her in his strong arms, positioning his face inches from hers. "And what a beautiful vessel she is."

"Oh, Cyrus, hush." Victoria giggled like a little girl.

Cyrus leaned into her, kissing her passionately on the lips. My blood boiled at the sight, but there was nothing I could do to stop it. I knew the attraction was solely between the demons, but it didn't make it any easier to watch.

Seeing movement out of the corner of my eye, I tore my gaze away from the disturbing scene. Jess and Melissa were tiptoeing around the perimeter of the cellar with what looked like pillowcases and some rope in their hands. *Where the hell did they find that?* They looked ready to kidnap someone rather than take down a demon.

I glanced at Cyrus and Victoria, who were still locked tightly together in a heavy make-out session. Swallowing the bile creeping up my throat, I crept over to the girls. Jess passed me a pillowcase and some rope, then pointed to a nearby pillar that supported the ceiling. When I gave her a confused look, she mouthed, *Tie them up*. While tying them up was a good way to keep them trapped to perform an exorcism, I don't think she fully took into consideration the insane amount of strength a demon possesses. But seeing no better plan at the moment, I nodded in agreement. I just wanted my Ava back.

I held up my fingers, signaling I was going to count to three and then we would execute the plan. Jess and Melissa each gave me a tight nod in understanding. Then I began.

One. . .

Two. . .

Three!

All three of us charged toward the demonic lovers. Jess and Melissa took on Victoria while I took Cyrus. It looked as if Victoria had been weakened from being thrown off guard as Jess and Melissa dragged her to the nearby pillar and tied her up with surprising ease.

"Jess, Melissa!" I called out to them as I fought to keep a hold of Cyrus. Derek was bigger than me to begin with. Add in the inhuman strength of a demon and I was virtually powerless against him. "Come help me. He's too strong!"

They rushed over to me. Jess took the pillowcase that was dangling in my right hand and shoved Cyrus's head into it. Melissa grabbed one of his arms, and we worked together, trying to bring him to the nearest pillar. His constant thrashing, however, made it impossible.

"It's no use," I told them. "Jess, go get that rocking chair."

She quickly brought the chair to us. Then she kicked Cyrus's legs out from under him, forcing him to sit down in the chair. From there, Jess and Melissa held onto him while I wrapped the rope around him, securing him tightly to the chair.

"Go get my backpack," I ordered to no one in particular. Jess darted across the room and up the stairs.

"They're going to break free," Melissa called out to me as the demons continued to thrash, putting strain on the ropes. She had to practically shout for me to hear her over the awful screeching and groaning noises they were making.

"No, they won't," I assured her. "I'll get them exorcised before that happens."

Suddenly the room became dead silent. Melissa and I looked back and forth between each other and the demons. Both of us were totally confused.

"Austin?" Ava's sweet but terrified voice called out to me. "Austin, where are you? I can't see anything!" She broke off with a heart-wrenching sob.

"Mel, babe, what's going on?" Derek called out cautiously to his wife.

"Oh, my god. We need to free them!" Melissa cried as she frantically pulled at the rope that was securing her husband.

"Don't!" I yelled, holding up my palm like a stop sign. "It's a trick. They're still possessed."

"Mel, don't believe him! Please help me," Derek begged.

"I-I can't." Tears glistened on Melissa's cheeks as she slowly stepped away from her husband.

"Austin, please let me go," Ava sobbed. "I'm sorry I hurt you. Please don't do this!"

"I got it!" Jess announced as she ran down the stairs. She rushed over to me and I snatched the backpack from her hands.

The heartbreaking cries and pleadings from Ava and Derek continued, getting louder and louder. I wanted nothing more than to believe it was all over — to untie Ava and hold her in my arms again. But I wasn't stupid enough to fall for their little tricks. Quickly I unzipped the backpack and dug through it. As I reached deeper into the bag, my hand touched the cold steel flask and I yanked it out. I stood and hastily opened the lid.

"Would you both just shut the hell up!" I shouted as I flung holy water upon the vessels.

Derek's and Ava's sad, frightened voices were immediately replaced by the tortured screams of the demons that resided within them.

"That's better," I said more calmly.

I remained in place, looking back and forth between the trapped demons. I hadn't the slightest idea what to do next. I'd never performed an exorcism on more than one at a time. Surely it was possible, but was it safe? If only I had an extra set of *knowledgeable* hands for this. . .

I looked at Jess and Melissa. It was a long shot, but I asked anyway. "Do either of you know Latin?" Both of them shook their heads. *No surprise there.*

"Well, are you going to exorcise them or not?" Jess asked impatiently.

"I-I don't know what to do!" I hated that my voice sounded so panicky. "I've never exorcised two at a time."

"Just pick one, you idiot!"

She was right — I needed to just pick one and get it over with. Cyrus was clearly the leader of the two, which meant he was stronger. I doubted my ability to get rid of him alone. He admitted feeling threatened by Ava's power, which meant I really did need her by my side for this.

I went over to my girlfriend and knelt on the cold, damp concrete floor beside her. "I'm sorry babe, but this is *really* going to hurt."

I splashed holy water all over her body, causing Victoria to cry out. Even though I'd learned from past exorcisms that the human vessel could feel everything too, I couldn't help but smirk triumphantly at the excruciating pain I was causing the dark entity inside.

"Exorcizámos te, ómnis immúnde spiritus." She writhed in agony as I spoke the exorcism prayer. *"Ómnis satanic potéstas, ómnis infernális adversárii, ómnis légio."* Black, smoky tendrils peeked out from underneath the pillowcase. The urge to grab them and yank them out was strong, but I didn't dare touch them for fear that they'd burn me. . .or worse, possess me too. *"Ómnis congregátio et sécta diabólica, in nómine et virtúte Dómini nóstril Jésu."*

I continued the prayer, occasionally splashing more holy water on her body. About halfway through, her agonized screams became muffled. Without stopping the prayer, I tore off the pillowcase. Ava's eyes darted around the room fearfully as she was being suffocated by the tendrils coming out of her nose and mouth.

The words spilled out of my mouth faster. I feared Ava would die if Victoria didn't leave her body soon.

"Váde sátana, inventor et magíster ómnis falláciae. . ." As I recited the last paragraph, the tendrils shot out of her orifices and slammed into the ground, vanishing upon impact.

I finished off the prayer and ended with one final splash of holy water to make sure Victoria was really gone. Ava's head lolled to the side with her eyes closed. Melissa got on her knees beside her and checked her vitals while Jess untied the ropes.

"She's still breathing," Melissa assured me.

"How long will she be like this?" Jess asked.

"Not long, I hope," I replied, glancing at the occupied rocking chair. "I don't think I can get rid of that one on my own."

Cyrus, who'd been mostly quiet the last couple of minutes, tilted his covered head and growled as if he knew I was talking about him.

"Oh, hush," I snapped. To my surprise, his growling ceased and the room became silent again — like the calm before the storm.

Suddenly, Cyrus began thrashing intensely. The rocking chair creaked and groaned, sounding as if it would break at any moment. He then growled and screeched like a feral animal.

"You have to do something!" Jess yelled above the noise.

Still unconscious, Ava was lying on the floor. I had no choice — I had to exorcise Cyrus by myself.

Moving as close to Cyrus as I dared, I recited the prayer once again. The ropes holding him down were being stretched to the max from his movements. Melissa and Jess ran over and attempted to hold both him and the chair in place. A splash of holy water halted his movements just long enough for them to get a good grip. Although they were unable to hold him completely still, at least the chair was no longer threatening to break apart.

A few sentences into the exorcism, the demonic tendrils began to seep out of the pillowcase. I paused, momentarily thrown off guard. *There's no way Cyrus is this easy to exorcise...*

I mentally shook myself and focused on the task at hand. Before I could finish another sentence, the tendrils shot out like rockets, leaving behind the foul scent of death and decay as they whirred past me. Derek's body instantly went limp in the chair. Melissa rushed to free her husband from the pillowcase and ensure he was still alive.

Jess eyed her dad suspiciously as she asked, "Is it over?"

"I, uh, I'm not sure," I replied truthfully, feeling more than a little confused. It definitely seemed over, but how? For Cyrus being such a big bad demon, he sure was easy to get rid of. I smirked to myself. *Or maybe I'm just that badass.*

"Um, A-Austin," Melissa stammered as she looked past me, her hazel eyes filled with horror.

"What?" I asked, turning around to look.

Ava was standing inches away from me. My blue eyes locked onto her black ones. One corner of her mouth curled up into a cocky smirk.

A voice way too deep to be her own snarled from within her. "You didn't really think you could get rid of me *that* easily, did you?"

CHAPTER FIFTEEN

"Oh, my god!" I groaned in frustration.

"God's not here, you piece of shit!" Cyrus yelled as Ava's fist connected with my cheek.

My head snapped to the side from the force. Heat radiated from my cheek as blood rushed to it. I felt liquid trickling down my face and rubbed at the spot. When I pulled my hand away, there was a streak of red on my palm. The temptation to swing back was strong as my anger reached an all-time high, but I couldn't allow myself to do it again — not if it meant hurting Ava in the process.

"What the hell do you want?" I shouted.

"What we always want," he replied nonchalantly. "Human souls."

"You've had plenty of chances to take our souls without all this bullshit."

Cyrus grinned darkly. "Oh, but where's the fun in that? I'll admit, I was getting rather bored of the humans living in this house and was ready to put an end to it all with Derek's shiny new toy upstairs." He let out a dreamy sigh. "But then precious little Ava returned and I just couldn't resist the urge to play some more."

"You're fucking sick," I hissed.

"Flattery will get you nowhere," he said with a hint of amusement. He snapped his fingers as he began to pace. "I've just come up with an excellent idea on how to make this even more enjoyable."

I narrowed my eyes angrily at him. Through clenched teeth I asked, "What could possibly be more *enjoyable* than this?"

"You see. . ." He spoke a little louder, showing his authority over the room. "Your little girlfriend here can see, hear, and feel every single thing going on right now." He paused to flash me a mischievous grin. "But you probably already knew that from your past encounters with my kind."

My jaw clenched and unclenched as a new wave of rage surged through me. Of course I knew that. Ava and I had performed several exorcisms in the past, and the humans would speak of their experiences afterward. They had just as much access to the demon's mind as the demon did theirs and experienced all the physical sensations of both human and demon — they just simply lost control of their body.

"Victoria was giving you the chance of a lifetime when she told you to leave earlier," Cyrus continued. "You really should have listened to her."

"I wasn't going to play into your little game."

Laughter exploded from him. *"Au contraire,* dear Austin. You played right into my *little game"* —he put air quotes around the words—"by choosing to stay here." He stopped pacing right in front of me, putting Ava's face mere inches from mine, and met my steady gaze. "Because now *I* get the pleasure of forcing your precious little girlfriend to watch you *die."*

Before I had time to react, Ava's hand wrapped tightly around my throat. I was hoisted into the air, my head nearly touching the low ceiling. Her face was set in an evil snarl as her hate-filled eyes studied me closely, watching the life slowly drain from me.

Tears streamed down my face as I realized I was soon going to perish at the hands of my one true love. I kept my eyes locked on her, trying to plead with the human soul buried inside — to give her strength to push past the demonic forces within.

"Ava, I love you," I managed through gasps of dwindling air. "Please do—"

The last bit of air had left my lungs before I could finish, and I was no longer able to take more in. My vision quickly began to fade, turning the world into a giant blur of colors. Just before my eyes drifted shut, I caught a glimpse of Ava's eyes beginning to change back into their beautiful hazel color. Her humanity was pushing through, sparking an inkling of hope that all was not lost.

"Austin!" I faintly heard a girl's voice shout my name as I landed on the concrete with a thud.

Air rushed into my oxygen-deprived lungs, causing me to gasp loudly. I was vaguely aware of a shadow looming over me and the girl repeatedly calling my name, but I was too exhausted to open my eyes or respond.

"Austin! Wake the hell up you moron!"

"Jess," I managed to mutter in annoyance.

Suddenly I was hauled into an upright position. I opened my eyes and blinked a few times to clear my vision. Jess's face was directly in front of mine.

"Get your ass up!" She groaned as she struggled to lift me onto my feet. "Your girlfriend is about to completely lose control. She needs you damn it!"

"Lose control?" I repeated, still feeling dazed and confused.

Once I was on my feet, everything began to come into focus. The first thing I became aware of was Ava doubled over on the ground, reaching for the flask of holy water that must have fallen from my hands when she was choking me to death.

The next thing I noticed was that she was muttering something to herself. I grabbed the almost empty flask and crouched beside her. Her hazel eyes widened in surprise at the sight of me. When she spotted the flask in my hand, she snatched it from me. Still on her knees, she tilted her head back and poured the rest of the holy water on herself. Cyrus screamed in agony from within her. Between the demonic cries, I heard Ava speak the familiar Latin prayer.

She's trying to exorcise herself!

"Help!" she cried, returning to the fetal position. "Can't. . .losing. . ."

Her plea was enough to kickstart my mind and body once again. I quickly began reciting the prayer, picking up where she left off. "*Ímperat tíbi Déus Pater; ímperat tíbi Deus Fílius. . .*"

Ava suddenly began to levitate. As she rose higher, her body rotated until her head was aiming toward the ground. The snake-like tendrils poked out of her orifices.

If Cyrus leaves now, she's dead.

Although her voice was muffled by the tendrils coming from her mouth, I could still make out the words she recited.

"Ava, stop!" I called out to her, but it was no use. "Jess, Melissa, help me catch her."

As we ran toward Ava, the tendrils shot out of her body. Gravity quickly took over and she began to fall, head first, toward the ground. I flung my body onto the floor beneath her. Her head was inches away from connecting with my stomach when Jess and Melissa caught her.

They worked together to lay her on the ground beside me. I sighed in relief when I saw her chest rise and fall steadily. She was still alive and appeared to be all in one piece.

"Ava, please wake up," I said. My hand was trembling as I brushed the hair from her clammy face and kissed her forehead. "Please, babe, I need you."

"Austin," Jess said, her voice shaking.

I looked up to see her pointing to something across the room. Hesitantly, I turned around to investigate whatever new tragedy awaited me. I let out a loud groan filled with a mixture of anger and frustration.

"You've got to be fucking kidding me!"

PART THREE
Ava

CHAPTER SIXTEEN

Wake up. . .wake up. . .wake up. . .

The familiar woman's voice in my mind continued on repeat, sounding more and more urgent each time. As I regained consciousness, my senses slowly awakened. The first to come back was my hearing. Austin was shouting, tearing into someone big time. While trying to make sense of his words, I became aware of a nasty metallic taste in my mouth.

Blood.

As my sense of feeling came back, I noticed a dull ache in my jaw. I felt the rock-hard surface beneath my unusually sore body. Cool air brushed gently against my skin, bringing with it the scent of floral perfume. *Where have I smelled that before?*

Slowly, my sense of sight returned as I opened my eyes. The dim light reached my exposed eyes, causing me to squint in discomfort. It was as if I'd been in the darkness for an eternity and was no longer accustomed to the light. I blinked rapidly as my eyes adjusted. Within a few seconds, the room around me came into focus.

Melissa and Jess were crouched next to me, looking off into the distance. I manage to pull myself upright and looked in the same direction. Austin was standing a few feet away. A possessed and tied up Derek glowered at him from the rocking chair, eerily reminding me of Nathan. Suddenly my memories came flooding back — from both before and during my possession.

Victoria was a pain in the ass, but Austin had gotten rid of her with no problem. Cyrus, on the other hand, was like no demon we'd been up against before. Simply using holy water and reciting an exorcism prayer had done virtually nothing except cause him severe pain. He was too powerful.

"My old mentor once told me that positive energies weaken negative ones. So it only makes sense that having good spirits hanging around could weaken the demon." Austin's words from earlier drifted through my mind.

I could still feel the presence of the good spirits roaming around the house. If what Austin said were true, then how was Cyrus still so strong? It was as if he had some sort of endless power supply or a magical protective shield that prevented him from being weakened.

The woman's voice whispered to me once again. *Corner. . .corner. . .*

An image flashed through my mind of Austin, Jess, and Melissa crowded together in a corner of the cellar. Victoria had been furious to see them there. . .but why? Furrowing my brow, I tried hard to remember, but all I got as a result was a sharp, shooting pain in my temples — no answers.

Austin and Cyrus were still focused on each other, getting nowhere with their verbal threats and psychological games. At least he was keeping Cyrus distracted. I motioned for Melissa and Jess to stay put, and then I quickly crawled across the cellar. Thankfully the pile of boxes had been scattered about, leaving me with plenty of opportunities to stay hidden as I navigated my way to the corner.

Once there, I spotted the old, abandoned dumbwaiter on the wall. The door was standing wide-open. I pulled myself up and peered inside. An unusual-looking sigil had been drawn in red on the floor of the dumbwaiter cart. As I studied the intricate swirls and shapes, I vaguely recognized some of them as symbols from a demonology book I'd read a while back, but couldn't recall their meanings.

Latin words outlined the circle. Translated, they read, "Endless wealth and endless power, for all the souls you may devour."

This must be what is fueling Cyrus's power and keeping him tied to this house, I thought. If that were the case, destroying the sigil should allow us to get rid of Cyrus. I searched my pockets for my knife, but it wasn't there.

Looking around, I spotted an old rusty padlock on the floor and picked it up. It was better than nothing. Using the rough tip of the shackle, I began scraping away at the circle. Over time, the paint had settled into the wooden surface, making it more challenging to remove. After several attempts, I made a small break in the outer edge of the circle.

"Stop!" Cyrus's deep voice echoed loudly throughout the cellar.

I whipped my head around to see him staring directly at me, eyes dark as night. The rage that overcame him as he realized his twisted games were about to come to a dead end allowed him to break free of his rope prison. Shoving Austin to the side, he stormed in my direction. The padlock shackle was getting warm from friction as I frantically scraped a line through the circle.

"No!" Cyrus screeched as the circle became disconnected, cutting off his source of power once and for all.

Jess and Melissa took his moment of weakness as an opportunity to wrangle him back into the rocking chair. They used what little rope was left to partially restrain him once again.

I ran over to Austin. Grabbing hold of his hand, I said, "Let's send this asshole back to hell."

His eyes shone with unshed tears as he smiled down on me. He squeezed my hand tightly. "That's my girl."

Together we faced Cyrus and recited the exorcism prayer for what we hoped to be the last time. About halfway through, smoky tendrils snaked out of Derek's body. It was obvious that Cyrus had been weakened greatly from the broken sigil, but he was still too strong for the prayer alone. I spotted the flask of holy water a few feet away but remembered I'd used the last of it on myself.

We can't do this on our own.

As if a higher power had heard my words, a bright light flashed behind our enemy. Time seemed to stand still as four figures stepped forward: two adults and two children. I gasped in shock and dropped to my knees. Tears poured down my face as I recognized the ghostly family before me.

"Carrie," I sobbed as the woman crouched in front of me. The scent of her floral perfume wafted to me, bringing back memories of the last time I saw her. "I-I'm so s-sorry."

"Ava, shh, it's okay," she said gently as her cold hand brushed across my cheek.

I shook my head wildly. "Y-you're d-dead because of m-me."

"Oh, honey, no. Don't blame yourself."

"I-I left you b-behind." My chest ached as the uncontrollable sobbing continued, making it hard to breath.

"Sweetie, Cyrus had overheard our phone call. By the time you arrived, it was too late. I was already possessed by Victoria. It was only a matter of time."

My forehead wrinkled in confusion as I tried to process her words. "B-but you seemed so normal."

"Yes, because that was part of their game. Victoria allowed me to appear normal to lure you in."

"They wanted to kill me," I stated, finally catching on.

Carrie nodded. "Ava, I'm so glad you ran out that night. You saved yourself. If you had stayed, you'd have been nothing more than another sacrifice."

"Sacrifice?" I repeated questioningly.

"The seal you broke was created by James Mason. He wanted wealth in dark times, so he made a deal with Cyrus," she explained. "But it came at a deadly cost. James could have an endless supply of wealth as long as he provided sacrifices — human souls — to Cyrus in return. James was desperate and willing to do anything.

To ensure he kept his word, the two created the sigil that gave Cyrus access to the souls of any humans that stepped foot in this house and unlimited power so he couldn't be destroyed when intelligent humans ultimately figured out the truth. . ."

"Like Austin and I did," I finished.

"Exactly."

"But James would be dead by now," Austin pointed out. "So the deal should've come to an end and the sigil should've been destroyed long ago."

Carrie tilted her head up to look at him. "And put an end to a lifetime of power and souls? Are you forgetting how greedy demons are?"

Austin shrugged and rubbed the back of his neck. "Right, yeah, sorry."

Carrie rose to her feet while Austin helped haul me back onto mine. Then Carrie motioned for Jess and Melissa to come closer.

Her eyes were sad as she spoke to them. "My family and I tried our best to warn you." She let out a small chuckle. "It seems you don't scare as easily as we expected."

"Sorry," Jess said sheepishly.

"Don't be," Carrie told her gently. She glanced at Cyrus, who was being silenced by Nathan's dead hand covering his mouth. Then she looked at Melissa. "Your husband will be just fine."

"But Cyrus. . ." Melissa started.

"Thanks to Ava breaking the seal, Cyrus is now weak enough for us to send him back to hell, never to return," Carrie told her.

"Us?" I asked.

"Yes, *us*," Carrie replied with a wink.

She walked over to stand beside Nathan and gave the twin girls a tight nod of approval. They placed their hands on Derek's possessed body. The demon inside writhed in pain from the positive energies flowing through it. Without being told to, Jess and Melissa followed their lead.

"Ava, Austin," Carrie called over Cyrus's tortured screams. "Finish that prayer!"

Together we stepped forward and placed our hands next to the others as we picked up where we'd left off with the Latin prayer. We were almost done when the tendrils began to suffocate Derek. Panic hit me as I feared that either Derek would die or Cyrus would leave just to possess one of us again.

Carrie, Nathan, Allie, and Riley each grabbed hold of the tendrils. As Austin and I spoke the final words to complete the exorcism, they pulled with all their might. The tendrils flew out of their vessel and disappeared into the ground, bringing the four spirits with them. Melissa and Jess quickly released an unconscious Derek and carefully laid him on the floor.

"Holy shit," Austin breathed in bewilderment.

"We did it!" I exclaimed, throwing myself into his arms.

"We sure did." He held me tightly and kissed the top of my head.

Jess looked around the room as if expecting something scary to jump out and grab her. "What happened to the ghosts?"

I closed my eyes and took a few deep breaths as I focused on the energies in the house. I could no longer feel any paranormal presence lingering around. "They're gone."

"Where'd they go to?" Melissa asked.

"I don't know." I replied, looking at Austin for answers.

He shrugged. "I've never seen this happen before."

"Maybe they were dragged to hell with Cyrus," I said. A lump formed in my throat at the thought of such a sweet, innocent family spending an eternity among such nasty entities.

"Or their spirits found peace once they knew the danger was gone," Austin added.

"I like that idea better," Jess said.

"Me too," I agreed, smiling at her.

Melissa put an arm around her daughter and looked at me. "So is it really over now?"

"Yes, it's really over."

CHAPTER SEVENTEEN

Tears of joy ran down our faces as the four of us gathered into a group hug. The Lloyd family was alive and well, Cyrus and Victoria were spending the rest of eternity in hell, and I finally got the closure I needed all along.

"Mel," Derek muttered from the floor.

"I'm right here baby," Melissa said as she knelt beside him.

Derek sat up and immediately took his wife into his arms, pulling her as close as possible. Crying hysterically, he said, "Mel, I-I'm so sorry. It wasn't m-me. You know I would never hurt you!"

"Shh," she soothed him. "I know, baby, I know. It's all over now, though. We're safe."

Derek let go of her and looked up at his daughter. "Jess, I've done nothing but push you and your brother away. Can you ever forgive me?"

"Of course, Dad." Her voice broke on a sob as she knelt beside her father and threw herself into his arms.

Austin tugged slightly on my arm and cocked his head toward the stairs, signaling for us to leave the room. The family needed a moment of peace together.

Once upstairs, I glanced out the front door. The moon was shining brightly in the night sky. Surprised that my phone was still in my pocket, I pulled it out to check the time only to find it had been shut off.

"Damn, it's almost midnight," Austin said, checking his own phone.

"Where's Brayden?" I asked.

"Melissa put him to bed earlier."

"I'm going to check on him," I said, starting up the stairs.

Austin followed me. "Hopefully the little guy slept through everything."

Once we reached the top, Austin walked directly to Brayden's room. I was getting ready to ask how he'd found it so quickly, but then I remembered he'd searched this floor earlier in the day.

Wow. Has it really only been one day? It felt like years had passed.

Austin and I peeked into the room. Brayden was curled up in his blankets with one arm draped over a teddy bear that was nearly the same size as him. Seeing how peaceful he was made everything else seem like nothing more than another nightmare.

Back in the living room, we waited patiently. A few minutes later, Jess, Melissa, and Derek stepped into the room. Although their eyes were red from crying, they looked to be in good spirits.

"Here," Jess said, handing Austin the backpack of equipment.

"Thanks."

"I should check on Brayden," Melissa said as she turned to leave the room.

"He's okay," I told her. "We just checked on him."

"He's definitely a heavy sleeper," Austin said with a laugh.

Satisfied with our update on their son, Derek and Melissa joined us on the couch. Jess took a seat in one of the chairs, turning slightly in it to face us.

"We can't thank you enough for all this," Melissa told Austin and me.

Derek nodded. "You saved our lives and that's a debt we can never repay."

"You don't need to," I ensured him.

"So this is what you do for a living? Hunt ghosts?" he asked.

"Yes," Austin and I replied in unison.

He let out a long breath. "Wow. I would have never believed any of this if I hadn't lived through it myself. This has definitely been an experience of a lifetime." He paused to chuckle. "Not that I'd want to go through it again, but it was an eye-opener."

All of us laughed. Then I said, "Lucky for you guys, Jess was a believer from the beginning."

"Yeah, if it weren't for her recognizing us from our videos, we might not have been able to save you guys in time," Austin added.

Melissa shifted her eyes to her daughter and grinned. "About that, you didn't really have an interview assignment, did you?"

"You know me so well," Jess replied with a proud smile plastered on her face. The room filling with laughter was a sound I wanted to hold on to forever.

"Well, it's pretty late now," Austin said once the room quieted down again. "I think it's time for us to head home." He looked at me hesitantly. "Unless I'm still supposed to go home alone."

"No way!" I wrapped a loving arm around him, resting my head on his shoulder. "Where you go, I go."

"Will you guys come back sometime?" Jess asked hopefully.

I smiled at her. "Of course. You have my number. Just say the word and we'll be here."

"How much do we owe you for this?" Melissa asked.

"Nothing at all," I told her. She began to protest but I raised a hand to stop her. "This was personal unfinished business I had to take care of. It wouldn't be right to charge you for it."

"Well, all right," she said, smiling warmly at me.

Melissa, Derek, and Jess walked us to the door. Before parting ways, we exchanged hugs and handshakes. The family thanked us for the millionth time. Then Austin and I stepped out into the cool October night air.

As we drove off, I spared one last glance at the house. No one was running after me, begging and pleading for my help. There was no dark cloud of smoke surrounding the house. There was nothing but a beautiful, old Victorian home with a safe, happy family resting peacefully inside.

I leaned my head against the seat and closed my eyes. A smile crossed my face as feelings of elation and freedom surged through me. Regret had haunted me for so long that I'd forgotten what it felt like to be free of such a burden. At last, the nightmare had come to an end.

EPILOGUE

Being possessed by a demon really takes a toll on a person — mentally and physically. Although I was able to leave behind the burden of the Johnson family's deaths, something else took its place. The memories of being possessed ate away at me daily. It wasn't just the fact that I'd broken Austin's heart and then nearly killed him. I also saw how dark and sinister a demon's life really is, and that in itself was the most traumatizing thing I'll ever experience.

I refused to talk with anyone about the impact it had on my life. It's not like any shrinks would believe me anyway. Heck, they'd probably lock me up in a padded room. Even though I kept it all bottled up inside, Austin could see how it affected me. That's why he made the decision for us to take a hiatus from paranormal investigating and go away together for a while.

Now, two weeks later, I stood on the deck of our vacation rental cabin in Tennessee, wrapped up in one of Austin's favorite hoodies. The setting sun shone brightly over the colorful trees that lined the sides of the Great Smoky Mountains. I took in a deep breath, letting the cool mountain air fill my lungs, and released a sigh of relaxation.

"Hey, babe," Austin said from behind me.

I turned to face him. "Hey."

He was wearing dark blue jeans and his hands were shoved into the pocket of his second favorite hoodie. As he got closer, I could see the almost fully healed cut on his cheek from when I had punched him while under Cyrus's control. My heart ached at the memory.

"I thought I'd find you out here." His blue eyes were full of concern. "Are you okay?"

"Yeah, just thinking."

He reached out to brush a strand of hair from my face. "About what?"

"About being possessed," I admitted shamefully. "I know I'm not supposed to think about it, but I can't help it." I threw my arms out to the side as the dam inside me broke. Tears of guilt and frustration streamed down my face. "I mean, shit, Austin. I broke your heart and almost killed you! How can I *not* think about that?"

"But you didn't," he reminded me gently. "You fought Cyrus. In all my years of doing this, I have *never* seen anyone fight against the demon possessing them like you did." He pulled me into his arms and sighed. "As for my broken heart, it's all better now."

I pressed my face against his chest and continued to cry my heart out. "The last thing I ever wanted to do was hurt you."

"*You* didn't hurt me at all." Keeping one hand on my waist, he used the other to lift my chin so my eyes met his. "In the end, everyone is happy." He smiled down at me. "And there were some pretty good things that came from all this too."

"Like what?"

"Well, for one, you got the closure you needed. What you thought was a mistake all these years turned out to be a blessing in disguise."

"That's true," I agreed.

"We also came out stronger in the end — stronger as paranormal investigators and as a couple," he added. "And I learned a little something throughout all of this."

I scoffed. "What? That our job will be the death of us?"

He chuckled. "That may be the case, but no." His face turned serious. "For a while there, I thought I'd lost you, and that was the worst feeling in the world. I learned that I don't want to live on this earth without you in my life." His brow furrowed slightly. "Well, okay, I suppose I already knew that. So I guess it just reinforced what I already knew, but—"

"Austin," I said with a laugh.

"Yeah?"

"You're rambling."

"Oh. . .yeah. . .right," he replied nervously as he took a step back and ran a hand through his hair. Clearing his throat, he began again. "Ava, I knew from the day I met you that you were someone special — someone worth caring for, loving, and protecting. I vowed to myself that, as long as you were in my life, I'd do whatever it took to keep you safe. I've tried my best to do just that all these years."

I smiled at him as a lump of emotion formed in my throat. We had known each other for nearly five years now. He'd spend five whole years trying his best to protect me without me even knowing.

"Two weeks ago, I thought I wouldn't be able to save you. I couldn't bear the thought of losing you — or worse, you roaming around hell without me." He flashed me the adorable cocky grin I loved so much. "I doubt you'd ever find someone as badass as me to protect you there."

He reached out and took one of my hands in his. "Learning all that I have recently, I would like to change my vow. I now vow to spend an *eternity* protecting you — to be by your side and follow you from this lifetime to the next. . .if you'll let me." He pulled a small black velvet box from his pocket as he got down on one knee. "Ava Moore, will you marry me?"

Despite all Victoria and Cyrus had made me say and do, I saw nothing but love as I looked deeply into Austin's eyes. It was clear to me that nothing — not even a super powerful demon — could tear us apart. This man was everything I'd ever dreamed of and more.

"Yes!" I screamed in excitement as tears of joy began to fall.

Austin slipped the silver ring onto my finger. The tiny diamonds sparkled brightly in what little sunlight remained. Then he stood up and wrapped me tightly in his arms.

I lifted my face up to his. "I love you so much."

"I love you too." His lips locked on to mine in a deep, passionate kiss.

We remained on the deck, wrapped up in each other's arms, long after the kiss ended and the sun had disappeared below the horizon. In that moment, life felt like a fairy tale.

Unfortunately, not all fairy tales have happy endings…

LOVED THIS BOOK?
SUPPORT THE AUTHOR BY LEAVING A REVIEW!

ABOUT THE AUTHOR

C. Smith has had a passion for reading and writing since she was a child. She can always be found with her nose stuck in a book or scrawling story ideas on a scrap piece of paper.

She is neurodivergent and has found writing to be a great form of self-therapy.

C. Smith grew up in Indiana and now resides near the beautiful Smoky Mountains in Tennessee.

SIGN UP TO GET NEWSLETTERS ABOUT NEW RELEASES, PRE-ORDER DATES, AND MORE